Innocent Bystander
An American Tragedy

Copyright © 2004 Steven R. Berger, Littleton, CO USA
All rights reserved.
No part of this book may be reproduced, scanned, or distributed in any printed or electronic form without permission.

This book is a work of fiction. Places, events, and situations in this book are purely fictional and any resemblance to actual persons, living or dead, is coincidental.

First published by BC Wryter Publishing

 TM

First Edition: May 2013
Printed in the United States of America
ISBN: 978-1-6203056-3-8
Library of Congress Control Number: 2013916650
Cover design: Jan Berger

Printed in the United States of America.

Innocent Bystander
An American Tragedy

by
Steven R. Berger

Dedicated to any poor bastard who,
though truly innocent,
has spent any time
incarcerated
or
who has had
to deal with the justice system.

Chapter 1

Pretending to be reaching for something under the front seat of his Ford Taurus, he watched with lascivious attention as Felicia Tafoya's long black hair swayed in syncopated opposition to her firm, round ass. "Oh, to bite that," he thought. It was bowling night, and now he was late. He would have to forego practice and limber up during the first few frames. He also needed to fib to his teammates, tell them he had to finish the monthly report for the paper supply house where he was comptroller.

Chuck Gray rarely lied. He worked at the same company for 19 years. He was still with his first wife, had a son and a daughter—both teenagers, and would have a dog if his wife wasn't allergic.

Felicia Tafoya was a co-worker who missed her bus, and would also miss her plane if Gray hadn't offered her a ride home to get her bags and catch a cab for the two- or three-mile ride to the terminal.

But, because his fellow bowlers, and fellow employees, would tease him about his "interest" in the *chiquita*, he was going to lie about where he had been, and what he had been doing. Especially since the division of labor at the giant wholesaler placed most whites in the office, and most Hispanics on the docks and in the warehouse, where a lot of young girls like Felicia worked. And there was June. He didn't want his wife of 22 years asking him where he had been and why.

Perhaps the only person he could confide in was Pete Winslow. They went back a long way. Chuck shared the grief of Pete's son's tragic death in a DUI car wreck two years ago. They played cards together with their wives. Reminisced about all the young girls they had before they were married—and an indiscretion or two that followed—and they bowled together on Wednesday nights.

Fortunately, Pete, Dave and Marty were in good form and carried Chuck until he warmed up. However, in the end, it still wasn't enough to beat Greg, Bill, James and Paul. Of course, it was the exercise and the camaraderie that mattered, not winning, or placing another trophy on the mantle in the rec room—though there was still time to make up for this one loss before the end of the current league season.

June was in the bathroom, leaning into the mirror and removing her makeup as Chuck entered the master bedroom. Bent at the hips, it gave him a perfect view of that little bulge beneath her navel, hips that had expanded some with the birth of two kids, and her derriere. Combined with her sensible medium-length light brown hairdo, she could never compete with the image that flooded the video screen of his mind with Felicia's perfect ass and long, black hair. Holding that thought, he gave June a soft and suggestive pat with his hand.

June smiled as she tilted her head down an inch while raising her eyebrows in a coquettish manner. "Didn't you get enough exercise tonight?" she teased as she wiggled her ass against his palm.

"There's always room for Jell-O," he replied.

"If that's what you think of my tush, then you can just go see what's in the fridge."

"Just kidding," he conjured up Felicia's round firmness and felt his penis grow into an erection for the second time that night.

* * *

Charles Stewart Gray would never be chosen for the romantic lead in a movie. More likely his ordinariness would make him a prime candidate for the CIA. Mid-forties, graying, thinning hair and a paunch from a lack of exercise. Complementing the entirely mundane ensemble, Chuck was exactly average height.

What he lacked in physical prowess, Chuck made up for in tenderness and devotion. However, tonight he had images of Felicia Tafoya imprinted on his psyche. He and June fondled one another as they had hundreds of times before. He caressed her the way a coat of varnish envelops a rare wood carving. Then he penetrated her like a piston in a well-oiled cylinder. Then, on her command, pumped her like a steam engine, held her arms down as he fucked and fucked and fucked.

Thoroughly spent, she murmured something about how she might not be able to sit down tomorrow; while he envisioned a pretty, small, brown body bejeweled with pearl-white drops of his semen.

Chapter 2

Sharleen Sicarian could always be counted on to add her assistance in any department at the paper supply warehouse. A liberal arts baccalaureate and an MBA combined with a strong sense of responsibility to make the administrative assistant a familiar face throughout the company. Hired as a secretary just three years earlier, it was now she who ensured that warehouse manager Jorgé Garcia had Felicia Tafoya's duties covered while she was on leave to visit her mother in Mexico. And, it was Sharleen who suggested Chuck Gray give the young woman a ride when she missed her bus.

It was also Sharleen who reviewed the numbers crunched by the comptroller and his staff before they were seen by company president, Bob Benton. She frequently screened Benton's appointments, proofread promotional materials for the company, approved decisions regarding policy, procedures and personnel made by the Human Resources Department, and even outlined content for the company newsletter. In fact, she was a more familiar presence in the company than Benton himself. Usually there when workers arrived in the morning, and frequently still at her desk as everyone left. So, it was no surprise that, when two plain-clothes police detectives arrived mid-morning on Thursday, they were shown to Sharleen Sicarian's modest, but central office.

"Good morning Ms. Sicarian," the first detective greeted her. "I'm Lieutenant Norman, and this is Sergeant Ives."

"It's Mrs.; nice to meet you both. Please sit down. How may I help you?"

"We're investigating a homicide that occurred early last night near the airport," Norman said without sitting. Reflexively he noted the neat stacks of paperwork on her desk, pictures of her children, a six- or seven-year-old in a frame from Graceland, an older sister in a frame from Disney World.

"That's terrible. What happened?"

"A young Hispanic woman."

"How could anyone...was she raped? What happened?"

"The coroner hasn't given us the details yet," Norman said. "For now, we would like information about one of your employees who was seen in the area last night."

"Of course. But how do you know it was one of our employees?"

"We were given a description of the car, and a partial plate. DMV gave us his name. His insurance records show that he works here."

"That's pretty amazing," Sharleen said, she was already thinking the dead girl might have a nubile young body and long black hair, and the suspect probably drives a late model Ford. "And, who might that be?"

"Charles Gray. We just want to ask him a few questions."

"That's interesting, Lieutenant."

"Why do you say that Mrs. Sicarian?"

"Well, last night, he took one of our other employees home. Felicia Tafoya. And she lives in that neighborhood."

Sergeant Ives was taking down the whole conversation in a small, flip-up notebook.

"How do you know this?" Norman asked.

"She missed her bus and, naturally, came to me. A lot of the girls here think of me like a big sister. I asked Chuck to give her a ride. He bowls on Wednesdays and I figured it wouldn't be too much out of his way. Also, he was the only one here besides me."

"How come you didn't give her a ride?" the sergeant interjected.

"Oh, I had too many things I needed to do here," she gestured at one of the neat stacks of papers on her desk. "Is Chuck a suspect?"

"Not at this time," the lieutenant said. "We just want to ask him a few questions. Maybe he saw something."

"Let me show you to his office. And, please, let me know if there is anything else I can do to help."

* * *

It was not unusual for Chuck Gray to receive visitors in business suits. However, none of them had been escorted by the company president's administrative assistant. And, no one could remember previous visitors wearing the plain black, utilitarian shoes of law enforcement.

"Chuck, this is Lieutenant Norman and Sergeant Ives," Sharleen Sicarian ushered the detectives into Gray's cluttered office. "They would like to ask you a few questions." She let the officers pass in front of her, but it was only after a look from Detective Norman that she retreated from her vantage point in the doorway. Ives gently closed the door for privacy.

"Please sit down. How can I help you gentlemen?" Gray asked.

"Where were you last night between 6:45 and 7:30, Mr. Gray?" Norman asked.

"It was my bowling night. I usually just go there straight from work," he tried to feel out what they were getting at, trying to employ tactics he had seen on television.

"But you didn't stick to your usual routine last night, did you?"

"Oh, last night. I gave another employee a lift home. Felicia Tafoya. Is there any problem? Is she all right?" he fumbled like a wide receiver with greasy hands. Why had he tried to avoid mentioning the detour he took on the way to the bowling alley? They knew about him taking Felicia home or they wouldn't be here. Sicarian must have confirmed that much.

"We don't know yet. There was some trouble over near the airport," Norman said as he watched for a reaction and noted the organized clutter of Gray's office, and the family tableau in a discount store frame. "We were wondering if maybe you saw anything peculiar while you were in the neighborhood?"

"What do you mean by peculiar?" Gray asked.

"A car or something you didn't think belonged there," the sergeant filled in without looking up from his notes.

"Maybe gang activity," Norman added, "or, you know, anything. Maybe even another late model car like the one you drive?"

"I know I didn't see any gangs or anything. And, I wasn't really paying any attention to the other cars," Gray answered honestly, wondering what his wife would think if she found out about this. Wishing he had told her something last night so she wouldn't think he lied to her—he just never mentioned the Tafoya girl. He just thought about her long hair, pert breasts and tight, little ass as he fucked his wife.

"Are you okay, Mr. Gray?" Ives looked up from his notebook for the first time.

"Oh yeah, sure. Thanks. Is there anything else?"

"Yeah," Norman continued. "So, if I understand you, you didn't see any other cars like yours, right?"

"Well, I can't really say."

"So maybe you were the only middle-aged, white guy with a young *chicana* and a newer car in that part of town last night?" Norman thought he had caught the scent. "And that no one would notice what was going on?"

"Wh..., what was going on?"

"A girl was raped and murdered?"

"Oh God. You found her?"

"What do you mean by that, Mr. Gray?" Norman sunk his teeth into the question like a pit bull with a steak.

"Huh? I don't understand."

"What did you mean by 'You found her?'" It was almost a growl.

"I meant, did *you* find her? Or did someone else find her? I wanted to know if you saw her? If it was Felicia?"

"You don't know?"

"Know what? Who found her?"

"No," the senior detective snapped. "You don't know if it was Felicia Tafoya?"

"No. Honest. I don't know who you found. If you were the one that found her."

"Found who?" The detective didn't like the way the questioning was going.

"The girl. Oh God. Whoever it was. Whoever found her. I don't know. Why can't you just tell me if it was Felicia?" Gray's anguish seeped out under the door. It wormed its way between the molecules of glass separating his office from the bullpen of bookkeepers outside. And it found its way to where Sharleen Sicarian pretended to be reviewing some paperwork.

"We can't tell you because no one can recognize the bruised face on the body. No one has found a relative with a strong enough stomach to ID the butt-fucked and bruised body," the bluntly graphic description stung the administrative assistant.

"Jesus Christ. Oh God," Gray held his head in his hands as his blasphemy became yet another dart piercing the sensibilities of Sharleen Sicarian. "Why are you doing this to me?"

"I think we better answer that question at the station, Mr. Gray."

"Sergeant Ives, read him his rights."

Chapter 3

Ridiculous things happen at the strangest times, like telling a joke at a funeral. For Chuck Gray it was the refrain from an old Nina Simone song he hadn't thought of in 20 years, "Go Limp." A humorous ditty from the civil rights movement of the '60s, it was the best advice he could give himself for the moment. Going limp would stop the chaffing of the handcuffs Sergeant Ives was obliged by law to put on him as he read Gray his rights.

Going limp might also mitigate the pain these same handcuffs inflicted as Lieutenant Norman found every bump and pothole in the city that would make the car bounce on its well-worn shocks.

Of course, going limp would do nothing to mitigate the humiliation Gray felt being led out through the bookkeeping bullpen. As he was paraded in front of his staff, and the ubiquitous Sharleen Sicarian, he felt totally naked. He just knew everyone could see his penis—purple as a plum from last night's love making.

His bruised self esteem also paraded past the wood and glass executive offices, the invitingly contemporary reception desk, and out the front door so every peer, secretary, dock worker and truck driver in the company could witness his shame.

Shit. Criminal. Rapist. Sodomite. At first, it seemed, they were trying to figure out what was happening. Then, recognition dawned like a curtain revealing a movie screen: it was Chuck Gray, the comptroller, the person who controlled the budget, recommended cutbacks and signed the paychecks. The one with the nearly new Ford. It must be embezzlement. Oh, if only it were true.

Then the looks changed, the bright awareness of autumn giving way to the moribund hues of winter. "Serves him right," the glares shouted. "Whatever the police think he did, they're probably right. The sonofabitch deserves it."

* * *

Even before Ives placed his hand on Gray's head to stuff him into the backseat of the police car, Sharleen Sicarian was in Bob Benton's office. "Bob, sorry to bother you, but we seem to have a small problem. The police just arrested Chuck Gray."

"Chuck?" Benton rose from behind his desk like a bear awakened in mid-hibernation. "What could he have done? I've known the man almost 20 years."

"I think it has something to do with a murder last night. It was out by the airport where some of our warehouse and dock workers live. You know the area?"

"Yes, yes. But why would Chuck be there? Doesn't he live near that new mall?"

"He was giving one of our girls a ride home."

"So what happened?"

"It seems that a girl was raped and murdered."

"Was it the girl Chuck took home? Is she here today? Wouldn't that clear up everything?" Benton asked.

"It would if she were here, Bob. But she isn't."

"She the murdered girl?" his voice as frail as an autumn leaf.

"It's plausible. Both our Felicia and the murdered girl were young Hispanics. But Felicia was on her way to Mexico to visit her mother. We don't expect her back until Monday. If she's ever going to come back."

"What can we do?" Benton was shocked by the prospect of someone he had known for almost two decades being a murderer, and worse.

"I'll take care of accounting for the time being," Sicarian volunteered. "And I'll call the airlines and contact Mrs. Gray. She's a teacher at the junior high."

"Good. Let me know what you find out," Benton said. "God, Chuck Gray. Who would think it?" he asked rhetorically.

"I suppose it's plausible," Sicarian answered anyway.

* * *

All Chuck Gray could think of as he walked along the puss-yellow walls of the local precinct station was that the handcuffs were probably making permanent scratches on the crystal of his watch. Of course, a gift from his wife, it would now bear the scars of his arrest. If only the scars could be contained on the watch crystal, the way Dorian Gray's trespasses were borne by his portrait.

But this was the real world, the crystal was scratched forever. But so too was that part of Chuck Gray the rabbi he rarely saw called the soul. "Nice fish," someone in uniform passing them in the hall said, "give him the chair."

Did the unidentified officer really know why Gray had been arrested? Or was this just occupational small talk? "We'll do that," Norman replied as if filling in the punch line to a favorite joke.

The hall was long and cold. Its putrid walls a counterpoint to the shit-brown floor. Overhead, neon tubes in sore need of new ballasts flickered like strobe lights. The catatonia-inducing light of the hallway shown onto a sizable room with a variety of old desks ranging from dark-stained pine monstrosities to dinged-and-dented metal obscenities. Of the dozen or so desks, nearly two-thirds sported computers. The scene would have been an anachronism, save that the computers had been ill-treated, each harboring a keyboard with the gray-grime of inconsiderate use feathering out from lettered keys and space bars to the black corruption of neglect.

Ives steered Gray toward a chair on the interrogate side of one of the large, dark, wood desks. Norman eased himself into a cracked-vinyl swivel number on its work side. Ives released the handcuffs and nudged Gray into the straight-backed wood chair. "Need me for anything, Bruce? I gotta take a leak."

"Go ahead. I'm sure this guy understands that he's Custer; and we're the Indians," Norman grinned.

"Let me see your driver's license, Gray," the lieutenant said as he brought the computer screen to full alert with the touch of a key.

"Everything here still correct?" Gray nodded, resolved to exercising his full rights by not saying a single word, except to ask for his lawyer.

"So, did you have a good time with that spic chic last night?" Norman asked nonchalantly.

"Huh?" Gray came back from a random thought that placed him somewhere far from this nightmare.

"You know," Norman said as he input Gray's vitals one slow key stroke at a time, "that Mex chic you took home. Did you have a lot of fun with her before you killed her?"

Despite his promise to himself to say nothing, Gray blurted out, "I never touched Felicia."

"But you did think about it, didn't you?" Norman looked from the keyboard into Gray's face and smiled.

"No. I'd never do anything like that."

"You'd never think of sodomizing her? Or you would never do it with any woman, not even your wife?"

"Do you have to talk like that?" Gray nearly whispered.

"Well, if the shoe fits..."

"I want to see my lawyer," Gray said firmly, finally composing himself.

Chapter 4

Last night June Gray thought it was a joke. But today, standing in front of her eighth grade history class, she felt the delightfully painful truth; she couldn't sit down for more than a few minutes at a time. It was all that passionate love making from her slightly balding, slightly paunchy and generally missionary-position husband. Especially his impromptu finale. Although it caused her a little pain and bleeding, and contributed the most to her discomfort, she couldn't say she objected.

It certainly wasn't consistent with the image her mother had when she named her only daughter for the pristine likeness of '60s television's June Cleaver.

She knew that at least 28 of the 30 students pretending to pay attention to her knew about sex—though she doubted they understood why most of today's lesson was taking place at the blackboard. Most picked up their sex education from peers or television, although a few actually learned about it from parents, books and the sex ed classes the prurient-right always want to cut from the curricula. Like if you didn't talk about it, it would disappear. Breasts wouldn't grow, pubic hair would stop its annoying progression toward loving bushes, and young, rampaging glands would cease secreting hormones. Ears would cease burning, armpits and foreheads would stop perspiring, diminutive, damp vaginas would dry up and little peckers would stop expanding into throbbing cocks. If fundamentalists really wanted to discourage premature copulation, sexually transmitted diseases, teenage pregnancy and sex crimes, they should allow that masturbation is natural and okay—because honey, nothing else is going to stop the flow of desire.

June Gray was somewhere in 1865—specifically in that five day period between Lee's surrender at Appomattox and the assassination of President Lincoln at Ford's Theater—when a girl in a neat skirt and white blouse slipped into her room and stood quietly against the wall, waiting politely to be recognized. Her status as an office helper was as obvious as color-coordinated bloomers were to a cheerleader.

The young lady held a note in her hand that might contain anything from an invitation to lunch with the school's principal to one of teacher Gray's own children having been squashed like a grape under an aberrant meteor. Suddenly all the aches between her legs disappeared in a flood of adrenaline. She moved unencumbered to where the girl stood and reached out her hand for the note.

"Thank you, dear," she replied evenly, although her heart pounded like a drum solo at rock concert.

Mrs. Gray,
Please contact your husband's employer as soon as possible.
Sara McNeil

The signature was from the principal's secretary. The history teacher had only gotten a message like this once before. And it led her directly to the hospital to wait for Chuck to come out of surgery for appendicitis. Now they were both in their forties, prime heart attack country. She'd been cutting back on the red meat and butter. Even on the margarine and cheese. Christ, was it all their activity last night—her body pulsated with tender pleasure for a heartbeat, just to remind her. Oh God, what if that was the last time they would ever make love? Thoughts careened through her head like roaches scattering in a sudden shower of bright light.

"Class, I have a small matter I must attend to right away," she controlled her panic so she wouldn't upset the children. Hell, she beat back her panic like a she-bear mauling the hunter that just wounded her. "Please open your books to chapter 26 and read quietly. I'll be back in a few minutes."

She was on Sara McNeil's phone, her knees weak as twigs. "I don't understand Mrs. Sicarian. There must be some mistake. Why would they want to talk to Chuck?"

"I'm sure it's nothing serious, Mrs. Gray. It's just because your husband was in a neighborhood where there had been some trouble last night. I'm sure they just want to ask him some questions about what he may have seen."

"What neighborhood? You mean where he bowls?" her hand went to the desk to steady the ever weakening twigs on which she stood.

"Out by the airport. He was there when he gave one of our girls a ride home last night," the executive assistant answered. "I think you should call the police right away Mrs. Gray."

"But if they only want to ask him some questions, why did they take him to the station? Why was he taking that girl home? I don't understand."

"Please Mrs. Gray, I can't help you. You will have to call the police. The number is 393-555-0126. Ask for Lieutenant Norman."

"Thank you," came the breathless acknowledgement.

"Sara, is there another phone I can use? Somewhere a little more private?"

"I've got to get today's attendance records. Why don't you just stay here and make your calls, June?"

"Thanks Sara," June Gray said as she fell into the secretary's chair like a piece of string.

Gathering strength from some unknown source deep within, she picked up the receiver again and dialed the number. "Lieutenant Norman, please. This is Mrs. Charles Gray."

"Mrs. Gray? Er? How can I help you? How did you...?"

Sensing the questions he didn't seem capable of asking, she said, "Mrs. Sicarian, where my husband is employed, called. I'm a teacher at the junior high. Would you please tell me why you have my husband in custody?"

"I can't discuss that over the phone Mrs. Gray. You need to come down here."

"Why can't you tell me what's going on? I'm Chuck's wife. I deserve an explanation."

"How do I know you are his wife? We can't just be giving out information over the phone to anyone who calls."

"Please, Lieutenant. Who else would be calling? Who else would have gotten a call from his company? We're not talking about national security, or even a celebrity murder. Damn it. We live at 1482 Carthay Circle. We have two teenage kids. Chuck drives a new Ford. He has a scar on his right buttock from a childhood injury and another on the right side of his abdomen from an appendectomy. How can I convince you that I am his wife?"

"You'll have to come down to the station and show us your driver's license, ma'am, or some other form of picture ID," he said, and then hung up.

"Shit," she thought, the phone still clenched in her hand, "now what?" Could she drive in her state? Yes. Driving would actually help calm her. Focus on the roads, the turns, the signals and stop signs. But what about the class?

"Are you going to be all right, June?" Sara McNeil asked as she re-entered her own office and heard the annoying recording from the phone company: "If you want to make a call, please hang up and try your number again."

"Oh. Oh God. Yes Sara, I'll be okay. But I have to leave school immediately. What am I going to do? I'm in the middle of a class," she said as she stood.

"It's okay, June," Sara said stepping closer and taking the other woman in her arms. "I can take over until the end of the period. And we'll work out something until we can get a substitute in here to help.

"Is there anything else I can do?"

"No. No thank you Sara. You're wonderful."

"Just let me tell Lamar what we need to do," McNeil told her as she ducked through the door marked Lamar Washington, Principal.

Chapter 5

"He lawyered up," Norman told Ives when the younger cop returned from the restroom. "Take him over to holding and book him. Then let him use the phone."

Ives held onto Gray's arm to steer him through the barred doors into the booking station. The comptroller was placed against a white wall with horizontal black strips to define his height. With a placard in front of him he was photographed. Then he was led to a chest-high shelf where Ives rolled his pudgy accountant fingers individually on an ink pad, and then immediately onto a paper form with Gray's name, address and other vital statistics. A pre-moistened towelette capable of cleaning a pinhead was handed to Gray to wipe his ten smudged fingertips.

He was then asked to empty his pockets onto a counter and to remove all jewelry. Each item was listed on an inventory form: wallet, keys, cell phone, pen, notebook, wristwatch and wedding band.

"Keep your pocket change, you'll need it for the phone. But give me your necktie, belt and shoelaces."

"I don't understand."

"It's procedure. So you don't try to hang yourself." Silently Gray obliged the officer.

Over by the holding cell there was a pay phone mounted on a wall. Gray couldn't believe he had to pay for his own calls. Why not just let him keep his cell phone? There were only a few quarters in his pocket, he prayed he would reach his lawyer on the first try. At least it was daytime, there would be a receptionist or secretary to take a message.

Shit. What if he had to leave a message? What would he say? How long would he have to be in jail? How long before he could talk with his lawyer? Would his lawyer call him back in jail? Would the cops let the call go through? What about his wife? Was there anyone who might give a rat's ass about him when they heard why he'd been arrested?

His first quarter clinked its way down the esophagus of the chrome and black box until it came to rest in some mechanism that let the phone company know it had collected its legal tender. One ring after he punched in the number, a very business-like voice came on with the law firm's name. "Hello, this is Chuck Gray, I need to talk to Michael Shapiro."

"I'm sorry, he's in a meeting," came the reply that Gray just then identified as male though effeminate. "May I help you? Is there a number where he can reach you?"

"Oh jeez. No. I'm in jail."

"I'm sorry Mr. Gray. Did you say you're in jail?"

"Yes, Goddamn it."

"Please wait. I'll find someone to help you immediately. Don't go away. I'll be just a moment, okay?"

"Yes. Yes. I'll be right here." Where the hell else would I be, he thought, but then was grateful for the man's judgment and quick reaction.

Gray held the receiver tightly, fearing that if he loosened his grip the open line would slip away like cooked spaghetti down the kitchen drain. Then he would have to use more of his precious pocket change to call back. And what if something happened to those coins? And the next try too? The receptionist didn't know where he was being held, or for what. Nobody would be able to help him. Didn't he read about people getting lost in the system? June would get home and make dinner for the kids and him, only he wouldn't show up.

At first, she would be concerned. Then scared, upset, pissed off, and then scared again. Jesus, what was taking so long? How long does the phone company allow a line to stay open without any activity? God, he wished they had some Muzak. Even those annoying, self-serving commercial ads would be better than wondering if the line had gone dead.

Finally, a voice came on the line, but it wasn't the receptionist. It was a woman's voice, "If you wish to make a call, please hang up and try again." Oh God. It happened. Stop. Take a deep breath. It's okay. Just take out another quarter and call again. This time tell the guy the number where you're at, just in case. Gray already had the quarter out, but his hand trembled like the tail pipe of a chopped Harley. It rattled against the slim opening of the coin drop, and when it finally fell through it was the most precious penetration Gray performed since the first time he got laid.

Again the slightly effeminate male voice announced the major partners for whom the law firm had been named. "Oh, thank God," Gray said.

"Oh, Mr. Gray, I'm so sorry we were disconnected. Let me put you through to Mr. Shapiro right away."

"No. I mean just a second. In case we get cut off again, I'm at..." there was no number on the telephone. "Oh shit. Someone took the number off this phone."

"It will be all right, Mr. Gray. We won't lose you again, I promise," the receptionist said just before putting Gray on hold.

The moments ticked away like tectonic plates moving apart over the millennia. There was a click on the line and he expected the saccharine, pre-recorded voice of the operator again. "Chuck? Tony just gave me the message. You're not really in jail, are you?"

"Michael. Thank God. Yes, it's true. I've been ah, ah, arrested," the word choked in his gullet and then finally Heimliched its way out into the world where it ricocheted off the puss-colored walls and reverberated back in his ears like a barred door slamming on his eternity. "I, I, I can't believe it. Jesus fuck. Michael, I'm in jail. Michael, I'm scared."

"Hang on Chuck. Take a deep breath. I'm sorry I have to ask you this, buddy, but does this have anything to do with embezzlement?"

"No. God, if that were only it."

"What is it then, Michael? Something domestic?"

"No, Michael. I think it's rape and murder."

"Oh fuck. Chuck, man, why'd the cops want you? You couldn't do something like that. What d'ya tell them?"

"Thanks for the encouragement, Michael. I haven't told them anything. It's my right, isn't it? I don't have to say anything unless you're here, right?"

"Absolutely," there was a subtle change in Shapiro's voice. Just one word, just a half note lower than the rest of their conversation. Shit, Gray thought. He thinks I might have done it. That's not good. My lawyer's got to believe in me.

"Chuck, you know I don't do criminal law. But my partner, Earl Levy, is great. Do you want me to talk with him?"

"God yes, Michael. I've got to get out of here. When can I talk with Levy? How soon can you get me out?"

"Try to calm down Chuck. Earl's out right now. I'll get Tony to call him on his cell. We'll see if he can swing by there before he comes back to the office. If we can get you out this afternoon, can you come right over here?"

"Yes, sure, of course. But I've got to call June. Is that okay?"

"Of course Chuck," the believable tone had returned to the attorney's voice. Gray wondered if he really believed in his client, or if some automatic reflex just kicked in. "I know it won't be easy, but try to relax. Do you do any meditating?"

"No, I never got into it."

"Well then, just try to stay calm. Maybe try to think of a really great time in your life, your honeymoon, when the kids were born, your last vacation. Okay?"

"Yeah, I'll try." Gray hung up the phone and thought about his kids for the first time that day. Yeah, when they were just born. Not as they were now, teenagers who seemed to disagree on principle with everything he and his wife said. And why? Because it wasn't cool. What would their friends think of them if they came to school like that?

Well, what are their friends going to think when their dad's face comes on the six o'clock news and hits the front page of the town's one remaining major newspaper?

Chapter 6

Tits. That's what the boys called them. Some of the girls did too. But they were the "bad" girls, the ones that let the boys brush up against them in the halls, and sometimes even more. Evelyn Gray and her friends called them breasts, the way you were supposed to. The way mothers and fathers and doctors and the evening news referred to them.

But in her mind, Evelyn liked to think of them as tits. Not teats. Pigs and cows and goats had teats, and all they were good for was nursing. Tits were for sex. When you said tits it was like a kiss. Short, crisp, stolen in a fleeting moment. It made her pink nipples erect with want. She fantasized a boy saying the word as he held one of her nipples in his teeth. And, it wasn't one of the boys she and her friends hung out with, not from the debate team, or even the football team. It was one of those guys that majored in auto shop. The boys her parents would make bring her home from a date at eight o'clock, if they let her go out with him at all.

She forced the veil no one else saw from her eyes and brought her attention back to her speech. She was running for president of that very same debate club whose boys didn't interest her. Although, since she was developing faster than most of the girls in her middle school, she was aware the boys were staring right at her full, 32-B, low-cut, lace bra behind a white rayon blouse. She convinced her mother that the lace bra was more comfortable than the stodgy cotton ones she had, and that she would only wear it with dark colors or a sweater. But her pride and joy, the envy of all her friends, was secreted out of the house in her lunch bag, and then she changed into it after gym to make her speech. It was the edge she felt she needed to win tomorrow's election, even though she was already favored.

As Evelyn took a deep breath to complete her speech, and fill her lacy bra to capacity, at the high school a few miles away her brother Zane, just 16 months older, toiled with biology. His pallor was very close to the color of the walls that surrounded his father in the jail cell of the precinct near the paper supplier where Zane, if he thought about his father at all, would think he was at that moment.

In addition to hating his parents for giving him such a lame name as Zane, the boy who swore to change his name to Zappa as soon as he was old enough, thought for sure that he must be adopted. How could anyone as cool as him have such dorks as parents? He grudgingly acknowledged that they probably had sex three times in their lives; himself, Evelyn and, he granted, their wedding night. Little did he realize how they had fucked their brains out the night before, much less why his father, if he thought of him at all, was not in his office at that moment.

Zane's color was a direct result of having just run a scalpel from the gullet to the genitalia of a frog. Bloodless gray guts appeared, framed by slimy green skin. Compounding the mucky texture and repulsive sight was the odor of fishy formaldehyde. It was enough to bring up his breakfast. But he choked back the equally distasteful bile, because he was cool. He turned his head to avoid the sight and inhaled the perfumed air that hung lazily about his lab partner.

Jenny wasn't his choice of partners. Sure, she was good. She should be, her father was a doctor. They probably talked about medical stuff all the time. But she was plain as a post. Even her tits, which had been cropping up on the other girls for the last two years, were lacking. Hell, his sister had bigger ones than Jenny, and she was just in junior high, he thought, guiltily recalling how he had "accidentally" walked in on her while she was getting out of the shower. What the hell, hadn't she walked in on him too, and did she stare at his penis? You bet. It'll be a long time before any of her friends can show her that kind of meat, he remembered thinking, and got a little erection from the memory of both incidents.

Chapter 7

"Bob? Do you have a moment?"

"Sure Sharleen. Is it about Chuck?"

"Yes. You asked me to let you know anything."

"Yes?"

"Well, Lieutenant Norman called me awhile ago. They've booked Chuck..."

"Did he confess?"

"No. Not exactly. The lieutenant said he clammed up like he was hiding something. He just asked to call a lawyer," the administrative assistant reported.

"Didn't they question him, you know, like on TV? Get him to say something, anything that might explain what happened?"

"I don't think they do as much of that kind of stuff in reality. Or at least not in this part of town. They just booked him and let him call his lawyer."

"Is that all the officer wanted to tell you?" Benton asked.

"No. He wanted to know if we could help him."

"What can we do?"

"He asked if I had heard anything around the office. I told him I hadn't, so he asked me to talk to some of our personnel. Find out what they might know about Chuck, his behavior, his background, anything."

"What did you find out?"

"Do you mind if I sit?"

"I'm sorry Sharleen, of course."

Her almost knee-length skirt road halfway up her substantial but attractive thighs as she lowered herself into a leather armchair across the glass-topped desk of her boss. Leaning forward conspiratorially and crossing her legs causing the skirt to inch up even more, Benton noted with satisfaction. "So what have you learned?" the CEO asked.

"According to the women in the accounting department, two ladies that used to work here said he touched them on different occasions."

"Wasn't that reported to their supervisor?" Benton asked.

"Apparently each girl did go and talk to Judy Marks about it."

"So why wasn't there any mention of these incidents in Chuck's file? Isn't the head of accounting supposed to report something like that to you?"

"Yes she is."

"So why didn't she?"

"I don't know. She's out sick today. Maybe she was afraid to report it, she works very closely with Chuck, and he is the comptroller. That makes him her direct supervisor."

"I hope you're wrong about that."

"Me too, it could leave us open to a sexual harassment suit."

"Do you think he grabbed a, ah, you know, touched them somewhere very private?"

"It's plausible, but none of the women here today seems to know what happened specifically."

"They never had any complaints about Chuck touching them?" Benton asked.

"No. But then the two that said they were touched were a lot younger."

"Oh, I see." Benton realized he actually did not see, since there was nobody in that department that turned his head. "Was there anything else?"

"Not really. Of course you've known that Chuck's real name isn't Gray, it's Grazinski. He's a Polish Jew."

"Oh, sure," the CEO lied. "Too hard to spell when you make reservations. Probably better for the kids in those suburban schools too."

"I guess. Unless there are some skeletons in the old family closet," Sicarian forced a laugh. "Anyway, those are the only bits of information I have. Do you think I should call Lieutenant Norman?"

"Did you try to call Judy Marks? Shouldn't we find out what really happened with those women first?"

"Of course. I'll do that right away. By the way, she's Jewish too. Maybe that has something to do with why she didn't report those incidents? Anyway, I think we should help the police, if it's at all possible. Oh, also, I called the school where Chuck's wife teaches."

"Did you tell her what happened?"

"I didn't tell her about him being arrested. I just gave her Lieutenant Norman's number and suggested she call."

"That was good. Thank you Sharleen."

* * *

Why did that little bitch have to call me in the middle of the day, June Gray thought as she pushed back tears of rage. This is probably nothing. Just some routine questioning because Chuck had driven through a bad neighborhood on his way to bowling. Damn. Who was she trying to fool? It wasn't Sicarian's fault Chuck gave that girl a ride. And it certainly wasn't Sicarian's fault something happened in that neighborhood. Good Christian woman she knew Sharleen Sicarian tried to be, she wouldn't have any idea what Chuck had done—June meant about him giving the girl a ride; not anything else that might have happened last night. It was just routine questioning she thought, as she cruised right through a red light without noticing.

But, why didn't that arrogant cop tell her it was just routine questioning when she called? What was this crap about having to check ID and see her in person? And what were those flashing red and blue lights behind her?

She pulled into the right lane and slowed down to let the motorcycle cop pass her. But he pulled right in behind her, and motioned for her to pull farther over. She obeyed his command, pulled out of traffic and stopped the car. What the hell did he want?

Did he know from her license plate she was the wife of someone being detained at the police station? Did he think she was an accomplice? (An accomplice to what?) Would he make her drive to the police station while he followed her?

She watched in the rear view mirror as the policeman switched off the ignition on his motorcycle. Then she got fidgety as he lifted a microphone and talked into it. "Come on, come on damnit," she whispered, "I don't have all day." Shit, he knows, she thought. This isn't right. I haven't done anything. My husband hasn't done anything. We're good people. Two great kids, a nice home, steady jobs. What was happening? She let just one tear escape her right eye. She wanted to just cry and cry until she could fall asleep. Then when she woke up all this would be gone, just a bad dream.

"May I see your license, registration and proof of insurance ma'am?" the officer asked politely. He appeared to her to be just slightly older than her son.

"Yes, of course officer," she said, taking her license from her purse before retrieving the other documents from the glove box.

"You know you ran a red light back at the intersection?"

"I did? I'm sorry officer, I was distracted. It's a family emergency."

"You better pay attention to your driving, or there will be another family emergency," he said without interest or emotion.

"Really, I need to get to my husband."

"Is he in the hospital or hurt?"

"Well, no but..."

"Then he'll be wherever he is when you get there. Please wait a moment," he said, and turned without waiting for a response. Back at his motorcycle he went through the procedure of calling her in. A process that is always tediously long became a surrealistic trip through the space-time continuum for June Gray. Finally, after the formation of several new islands in the Pacific and a three-degree rise in global warming, he returned.

She half expected him to comment on her "fugitive" husband, but instead he just returned her papers, had her sign the traffic ticket and said, "Better keep your mind on your driving, Mrs. Gray, or your husband will be waiting a very long time for you." Very funny, she thought, I ought to take you over my knee and spank you. But you would probably enjoy it in your little Gestapo uniform with your shiny handcuffs.

Like the newly converted, she crept along at a parson's pace for the next two or three miles. Never exceeding the speed limit, coming to complete stops at stop signs and watching for red lights like a john in the tenderloin.

Chapter 8

Chuck Gray, a.k.a. Charles Grazinski, had just enough coins left for one more phone call. His lawyer, or more specifically, his lawyer's partner, the "criminal" lawyer, was on his way. He didn't know if he should call his wife or hold onto the quarter in case he needed it for another call. An astute comptroller and CPA, a fiscal conservative to the end, he left the quarter in his pocket. He could always ask his lawyer to call his wife. Besides, June was better off not knowing. What good could she do? It would be better for her to just continue her duties uninterrupted at the middle school.

"You done with the phone?" the booking sergeant asked.

"For now," he said with the conviction of a hung jury.

"Come on then, let's get you into the cell."

The cell? They were going to lock him up in a cell with real criminals? Thoughts rampaged through his brain like a heretic in the Vatican. The first organ affected was his mouth, his tongue swelled up like a balloon in a toilet paper roll. All the moisture in his mouth dehydrated away like a mist in the Sahara. Even if he were capable of forming a coherent thought with his addled brain, he couldn't talk.

The next organs to betray him were his sphincter muscles and his bladder. The one tightened up involuntarily while the other suddenly made him aware that he hadn't urinated in hours. "I, I have to go to the bathroom," his voice dribbled out.

"What?"

"I need to pee. Can I go to the bathroom before you lock me up?"

"There's a head in the cell. Come on." Again he was taken by the bicep and wheeled though the opening in the steel bars into a 16 x 16-foot area. The holding cell had bars on two sides and concrete walls on the other two. The walls were the same puss color as the rest of the precinct. But the combination of moisture from eight men breathing, sweating, urinating and defecating, added a slimy sheen to the glossy paint that gave it a coating like a glazed donut.

"Here, you can take a piss in the corner," the officer jerked back on Gray's bicep to force his attention toward the stainless-steel, seatless toilet in the corner.

The dread brought home by a solitary stool out in the open was no less a contrast in realities for Chuck Gray than the obvious differences between his twill trousers, clean cotton shirt and polished wing-tips and the grungy jeans, odoriferous tee shirts and scuffed footwear of his cellmates.

"Fresh meat," the officer said, releasing Gray's arm and locking the cell door behind him. The phrase rolled around inside Gray's head, ricocheting off the inarticulate thoughts of what was happening to him. How did he come to be here? What did that cop just say? If only he hadn't given Felicia with the delicious ass a ride home.

He did, he did say, "Fresh meat," the sound finally hit home. But no one seemed to care. They all just huddled in twos and threes, most of them smoking and talking. That was a relief. They didn't seem interested in him at all. He still had to pee. He wondered if he could. Sometimes he couldn't even get his stream going in the semi-privacy of a men's room.

He tested his bladder first, just relaxing enough for a little drop to ease out into his shorts. Yes, he could do it. He hadn't pissed in several hours, and there had been much coffee to join with the milk on his cereal. This would be good, it would make him feel better. He walked over to the bowl reaching toward the zipper as he approached. But then he began to smell it. Urine and feces. His nostrils flared and his stomach churned, and then he looked down into the mess of toilet paper and turds.

He backed off, but then felt the need to pee even more. He approached, held his breath and reached down to flush. Suddenly everyone was looking at him. "Hey fuckface, what're you doin?" a large man with a protruding gut challenged.

"Jus..., just flushing."

"Who told you you could flush?" the man lumbered toward Gray like a tyrannosaurus. "Was that your shit?"

"Uh, no. Uh..."

"It was mine, asshole. I was saving it. Now you gotta put it back." The other inmates were smiling at the confrontation.

"Yeah," another man said. "It ain't yours. You gotta replace it."

"That's right," another spoke up.

"Uh huh," came a small chorus.

"Now, park your ass on that throne until you've replaced every single turd, you turd."

"Please, don't," Gray pleaded. "I didn't know, I've never been in jail before. I promise I won't do it again. Please."

"Gee, ain't that too bad," Tyrannosaurus said moving closer, "but we all gotta learn sometime. Drop those draws and ass-kiss the steel, now."

Suddenly there was something blocking Tyrannosaurus. He wasn't bigger than the behemoth, it was just the perspective of being between Gray and the bigger man that blocked him out. "Leave him alone," Gray heard his savior saying. "You heard him, he's new here."

Surprisingly the bigger man stepped back. "Oh, I didn't know he was one of your girls," Tyrannosaurus said. "Maybe later you'll let me watch you play kissy face."

"Back off you ox," Gray's savior said, "or I'll kiss you."

"No way, you butt-fucking plague," and Tyrannosaurus rejoined the men he had been with before. "Gimme a cigarette," he told one of his pals.

"Thank you," Gray said, noticing the man for the first time. Although well-built and taller than Gray, he was no match for Tyrannosaurus. "How come he listened to you? Weren't you afraid? Do you know karate or something?"

"No, I have AIDS. He's afraid I'll spit on him." It was just then that Gray noticed an angry sore through the open collar of the man's shirt.

"But you can't get AIDS like that," Gray whispered so he wouldn't lose his tenuous advantage.

"You and I might know that, but that dumb ox doesn't."

"How'd you get AIDS? Was it a transfusion or something?" Gray noted that the man didn't look the least bit effeminate.

"I'm gay."

"Oh. Uh …"

"Don't worry about it, you're not my type.

"So, it's always the same old question. What are you in here for?" the tarnished savior asked Gray.

"It's a mistake. I didn't do anything. I'll be out as soon as my lawyer gets here."

"Yeah, we're all innocent. So what kind of a mistake did the cops make with you?"

"I was in a neighborhood where a woman was raped and murdered. For some reason, they think I had something to do with it."

"You? Well, I guess you can't tell a book by its cover. I hope you used protection."

"But it wasn't me."

"Oh, yeah, of course not. They got me for creating a public nuisance."

Gray really wasn't interested, but he wanted to take the conversation away from himself, "What did you do?"

"Oh, I was just hanging out, having a beer. I'd taken a Vicodin and was just waiting for the buzz when a police cruiser came around the corner. I panicked a little because I had more dope on me. I pulled the other two tabs from my pocket and popped them with the rest of my beer."

"Won't that make you sleepy?"

"Yeah. I figure I have about 15 more minutes before I nod out."

"But, if they didn't arrest you for the pills, why're you here?"

"Oh, they wrote me a ticket for drinking in public. And, I asked them if I could say something."

"Yeah?" Gray asked.

"They said okay, so I said 'Ah fuck,' you know, really loud, and then they busted me for being a public nuisance. Hey, if you don't mind, I'm just going to lie down here for a few minutes," the man laid down on his side on the concrete floor by the bars, and in a moment was sound asleep.

As the man's breathing assumed the regularity of sleep, Tyrannosaurus looked over toward Gray and smiled his hideous intent. And warm pungent urine trickled freely down Gray's leg.

Chapter 9

As Gray cowered in his communal cell with warm urine turning cold all the way down his leg and into his shoe, a BMW and a Nissan Sentra pulled into the precinct's parking lot. The trim attorney in his Armani suit gracefully emerged from his car in time to hold the door on the Nissan open for the attractive woman in the fashionably demur outfit of someone who needs to promote the image of wholesomeness; a look the attorney had lusted after ever since he glimpsed his first non-familial cleavage on his well-endowed fifth-grade teacher.

"Thank you," June Gray proffered, mentally running a Dunn & Bradstreet on his accoutrements as well as an inventory of his physical assets. She brought herself back to reality, turned to grab her purse and walked before him toward the main entrance.

Noting her puffy eyes he said, "If you need any assistance, I'm an attorney. My name's Earl Levy."

She slowed her pace and let him move up beside her. "Thank you Mr. Levy. I'm here to see my husband, and I believe he already has a lawyer."

"Yes, of course. Well, I hope it's nothing too serious," he said reaching inside his breast pocket and producing his card. "Should your needs change, please give me a call," he said handing her the card.

Despite herself and her situation, she found something provocative in the way he said, "Should your needs change." Was he really inferring something more than legal advice, she wasn't sure. It would be presumptuous of him, of course, but she wasn't sure that she was offended.

In silence she passed in front of him as he held the door for her. He respectfully stayed a few paces behind as she approached the duty sergeant's desk. He remained silent as she told the sergeant she was there to see her husband, Charles Gray.

"It will be just a moment, Mrs. Gray. Please have a seat and I'll call you when we've moved him into a conference room."

"Thank you," she replied, as meekly as her below-the-knee skirt and criss crossed polyester blouse would have said.

"Yes sir?" the sergeant turned his attention to Levy even before June Gray had begun to move.

"I'll be with you in a moment, sergeant," Levy said in a voice that carried neither rancor nor innuendo, but still commanded as much respect as a room full of generals.

What a fortunate coincidence, he thought, turning to follow his client's wife to a bench by the wall. "Mrs. Gray?"

"Yes?" she turned toward him before sitting. It was like a scene in an old Bogie flick. She was Lauren Bacall, clutching her purse in both hands, looking up at his face nearly a foot above hers. He was Bogart, his arms at his side, holding a briefcase in one hand. They were so close together their shadows were already making love.

"It seems we have something in common," he said without revealing his thoughts. "Your husband is my client. Michael Shapiro and I are partners. He does family, estate and general law. I do crim... , well, he asked me to represent your husband."

"Oh," she cooed. And without the training of a litigator, she gave away her desire in a single syllable.

"Is there anything you want to discuss with me before your husband can see us?"

"Uh, no. I really don't know what's happening," she took a step back, perhaps to escape the heat building up below her navel. She looked around for the bench and let herself down slowly.

"Do you need a hankie?" he asked, and actually produced a silk handkerchief from his pocket.

"No, I'm all right. I was at school, I'm a teacher, and I got a call from someone in Chuck's office. Her name's Sicarian, Sharleen Sicarian. She didn't tell me much. Just that Chuck was being detained, and that I should talk to a Lieutenant Norman.

"But, if you're here, it must be more serious than they said. Oh God. Is he all right? What's happening?" she grabbed the handkerchief from his hand and sobbed into it.

"It's going to be all right, Mrs. Gray," he said sitting down beside her and placing a hand on her hunched-over shoulder.

"I, I can't believe Chuck would do anything wrong. He's such a gentle man. Everyone likes him. He wouldn't hurt a living thing."

"I'm sure it's just some mistake," Levy told her. Yeah, he thought, just like John Wayne Gasey and Ted Bundy. But even psychopathic cretins deserve legal council.

"Sergeant?" The uniformed man turned around fast as a foreclosure. "I'm Earl Levy, Mr. Gray's attorney. When he's available, I'll be joining Mrs. Gray in a conference room. And, I'll want a copy of his arrest report as soon as possible."

"Yes sir," the sergeant replied.

"Will that be all right with you, Mrs. Gray? I know the two of you will want to see each other immediately, but I also think it would be prudent for me to see him as soon as possible."

"Yes, of course, thank you Mr. Levy."

"Please, call me Earl."

"Okay. Earl." She looked up from the handkerchief and saw exactly what she wanted to see. "I'm June."

"Mr. Levy, Mrs. Gray, Corporal Andrews will show you to the conference room."

"And the file, sergeant?"

"Right here, sir."

* * *

It was amazing how fast urine had gone from the comfortable temperature of the body to chilling cold. One would have thought that it would still be temperate by the time Tyrannosaurus began to move across the crowded cell toward Chuck Gray. "Okay fuckface, now that your fag friend has decided to take a little nappy, I want you to strip and sit until you shit. Do you understand me?"

"Please mister. I'm sorry. I didn't mean anything. I didn't know it was yours."

Tyrannosaurus still had his grin plastered on. Gray didn't understand that this had nothing to do with him flushing the toilet. It really didn't have anything to do with Gray at all. It was just posturing and pissing away the time. Gray might have been a five-legged cockroach Tyrannosaurus was racing for toothpicks. He might have been a rat the inmates were taunting with stale cheese and arsenic, he could even have been the receptacle of their sperm. However, it wasn't sex or possessions or even personal, it was just like politics and mega-businesses, driving the hard-deal, the hard-line and the hard-on to see who was the most powerful sonofabitch on the block.

"Move over there," Tyrannosaurus commanded. Gray moved away from the prostrate form of his one time savior. Without taking his eyes off his nemesis he inched his way crab-like over to the disgusting toilet. "Good, good. Now drop trou and sit."

"Huh?"

"Come on fuckface. Drop trou. Now." Gray unbuttoned the top of his pants and took hold of his zipper. "Now, godamnit. You don't want me to come over there and have to strip you." Gray pulled the zipper down, then pulled his pants down revealing colorful boxer shorts.

"Hey, fancy pants," one of the other men said. "Your mamma dress you today?"

"Now sit."

When Gray's cheeks felt the bitter cold of the steel rim, his balls drew up inside him as though he had been shoved into a cold shower.

"Gray. Charles Gray?" a uniformed officer called from the other side of the bars.

"Here. Uh, that's me," Gray tried to call from his corner in a voice that cracked with fear and the discomfort of his ascended testicles.

"Gray. Charles Gray," the officer's voice was edged with impatience.

"Mm, me." Gray called out, "that's me," he got up and nearly tripped on the clothes gathered about his knees.

"Well get you ass over here, your wife and your mouthpiece are here to see you."

"Oh..." he said aloud, and swallowed the "thank God" as he pulled up his pants and crossed to the cell door.

"See you later," Tyrannosaurus said.

Chapter 10

Earl Levy noted with satisfaction that the conference room had no mirrors. He didn't think the police in this precinct would underestimate him by having him confer with his client in a room where they could watch every eye flicker and knee jerk, as well as hear every word. In fact, the only glass in the room was a window, appropriately secured with a heavy, chain-link grid outside. This visual breath of fresh air among the putridity of the walls was like a blooming rose bush amid the offal of a dump site.

June Gray didn't seem to notice the difference between the waiting area where she had been with the nice smelling lawyer, and the room which they now shared, waiting for her husband. Who would have thought, she thought, that the same man who made passionate love to her last night, who worked his way up in the same company for nearly twenty years and attended all of their son's little league games and all of their daughter's dance recitals would be incarcerated? Locked up, she imagined, in a small cell with two bunk beds and a big burly cellmate who would show him the ropes. God, she thought, I hope that's all he shows him.

No, the room meant nothing to her. Everywhere she had been in the last two hours was the same. On the phone, in the principal's outer office, in her car, getting a ticket for running the red light, waiting with Levy out by the desk sergeant's area, and this room. Everything was shrouded in a gray pall, except for that one shining moment when the attorney looked deep into her eyes from the vantage point of his six-foot frame. He aroused her in more ways than one, in more ways than her husband had in all the years of their marriage. She let her mind drift back to that instant only minutes ago. She bathed herself in that safe and luxurious moment as she looked at the attorney. He ventured a glance up from the file folder that held his attention and smiled.

"Are you going to be all right?" Levy asked.

She nodded.

"This is much more serious than I thought."

She nodded again.

"There was a rape and murder last night. Your husband's car was seen in the area."

She nodded.

"According to Mrs. Sharleen Sicarian, the administrative assistant to your husband's boss, your husband had given a lift to a Hispanic girl that works with him. Her name was Felicia Tafoya. Do you know her?"

"No," her answer was as quiet as ink drying.

"Did your husband ever mention her?"

"No."

"Did you know he gave her a ride home last night before going bowling?"

"No."

"And, the neighborhood where the rape and murder occurred is over by the airport, not exactly on the way to the bowling alley.

"The girl, Felicia Tafoya wasn't at work today, but Mrs. Sicarian didn't expect her back until Monday. She was going out of town to visit her mother."

"Poor girl."

"They're not certain that she's the one murdered. Delicately put, no one has identified the body."

"Then, they can't be sure that Chuck had anything to do with it," June Gray said, becoming animated for the second time since she met the lawyer.

"I don't want to dash your hopes, Mrs. Gray. But, even if the girl isn't this Felicia Tafoya, your husband was still in the wrong place at the wrong time."

"But Chuck would never do anything like that. Not to the Tafoya girl, not to anyone. Why he doesn't even notice other women," a twinge of guilt flickered through her like a feather bussing her inner thigh. "He's a good father and a good husband."

She had him going for a minute. Until she mentioned his not even noticing other women. The lawyer had yet to meet the man who didn't take note of other women. Only some felt that by hiding it they might enhance the image of their own fidelity.

"Oh, darling," June Gray gushed as she rose from her seat like a geyser. She took a few uncharacteristically long steps toward him and threw her arms around his neck. He reciprocated by enfolding her in his arms as the policeman that escorted him in backed out of the room. "Oh Chuck, oh Chuck. Are you all right? What's happened? There must be some mistake."

"Oh, thank God June. Yes, yes, there's been some mistake. I don't know what happened. Last night, I'm sorry. I should have told you I took that girl home. But that was all. I swear, nothing else happened. She was late for a plane or something, and had missed her bus."

"See, Mr. Levy. I told you it was all a mistake. Chuck wouldn't hurt anyone."

"Mr. Levy? Michael Shapiro's partner? How did you two meet? Who told you I was here?" he directed his last question to his wife.

"Mrs. Sicarian called me at school."

"Of course, she would want you to know right away," Gray said as he broke free of his wife. "Mr. Levy, I'm so glad you're here. Can you get me out? There must be some mistake. I can't stay here. It's awful."

"Please, Mr. Gray, sit down, we need to talk. I won't be able to get you out until you are arraigned. And call me Earl."

"I'm so glad you're here, Earl. And you too, honey. Can I stay here with you two until the arraignment?"

"I doubt that. Has it been rough on you?" For the first time Mrs. Gray noticed the rank smell of urine on her husband, and his shabby appearance.

"My God, Chuck, what have they done? Mr. Levy, you can't let him go back in there. There must be a way to keep him out. Can't we post bail?"

"I'm sorry Mrs. Gray," Levy said, even in the light of dealing with a tragedy, he was sadly aware their relationship had lapsed understandably back to the formal, a hint that his advances had not gone unnoticed, or unappreciated. "In a felony case like this, bail won't be posted until Chuck is arraigned."

"But he's innocent. Look at him. He wouldn't hurt a soul. He can't go back in there," her words came fast and strong like the swat of a she-bear. Still, the attorney knew that looks meant nothing, to a judge, jury or himself. However, he did have to admit that the man didn't look like he would last another five minutes in the holding cell.

"I'll see what I can do, Mrs. Gray. Would you like a few minutes alone before your husband and I talk?"

"I want to stay," she said.

"I'm sorry Mrs. Gray, I need to talk with Chuck alone. Please, it's for the best. I'll leave you alone for a few minutes, then Chuck and I need to talk," he said soothingly.

Trust enveloped her like an electric blanket on a cold night, "Of course. We'll just be a few minutes."

When the door clicked shut behind the attorney, June Gray turned gently toward her husband, "Oh Chuck, how could this have happened? Why did you have to take that girl home? How come you didn't tell me about her?"

"I'm so sorry June. I was just trying to do her a favor. She works on the docks, she missed her bus and had to catch a plane. Apparently she went crying to Sharleen, and Sharleen asked if I could give her a ride on my way to bowling."

"Sharleen knows about your bowling night?"

"Everyone knows about my bowling night. Besides, Sharleen makes it her business to know about everything. You know that. Anyway, she asked me, and I felt sorry for the girl and gave her a lift. But that's all, I swear. The last time I saw her she was walking up the steps to her house."

"Why didn't you tell me about her last night?"

"There was nothing to tell. It meant nothing," he told her. "It was just one of the people I work with needing a favor. It could have been Jack or Jesus or anyone," but he was sure the sight of their asses swaying rhythmically up the walkway wouldn't have given him an erection.

"Oh God, Chuck, I know, I'm sorry. I'm just so confused. I just wish you weren't so nice," and she gave him a hug despite the smell. "You better talk with Mr. Levy. I'll... Oh, God, I don't know what I'll do Chuck. Shit. Why did you have to go and get yourself arrested? Everything was going along so well. You've got a good job, I'm doing okay at the school, the kids are happy. Shit, Chuck, why did you have to go and screw it all up?

"Oh God, I'm sorry Chuck. I'm so sorry, I just don't know what to do. Please forgive me, I shouldn't have said what I said, poor Chuck, you're a mess," she reached out both hands and straightened the drape of his shirt. "Where's you tie? You were wearing a tie this morning. And your belt? What's happening?"

"It's okay, June. You're just scared," he replied tenderly. "I'm scared too. Don't worry about the tie and belt, I had to give them to the police with my wallet and other stuff. I'll get them back. Levy will get this all straightened out. I love you."

"I love you too, Chuck," she sobbed into his chest.

Chapter 11

There was still a rumor of June Gray's perfume in the small room where Chuck Gray and Earl Levy sat. The pleasant smell would dissipate like a good idea in a committee, but for the few milliseconds it persisted, it caused both men to miss her.

"How're you doing?" the attorney asked his new client, even now, between the soft reassuring tones, he was sizing the man up. He appeared to be everything that his partner, Michael Shapiro, said he was. A character reference that was reinforced by Gray's wife. Levy had met some really gullible ones, some that were just plain stupid or fatally co-dependent, but none of those convenient though deficient terms described June Gray, he thought. Sure, she was caught in an emotional whirlpool, one that was bringing her down and down into a vortex of despair. But she would know if her husband was fucked up enough to trash another human being. Unless, of course, the formidable attorney's own longing for the prim but smoldering Mrs. Gray clouded his judgment.

Levy inhaled a discreetly deep breath, trying to ensnare the last lingering pheromone, "Mr. Gray? Chuck? Are you all right?"

"Sorry, Mr. Levy. I just can't believe this is happening to me."

"It's Earl. I understand Chuck," Levy told him with compassion and honesty. He had spent a night in jail as a juvenile for having a bottle of booze in his car. His parents were out of town so there was no one available to post bail for his misdemeanor until the next day. And, while his father had always wanted him to become a lawyer, it was that night of hell that did it. Earl Levy swore there was nothing worth going to jail for. "Iron bars *doth* a jail make," became his creed. Because when you're in jail, you can't be where you want to be. And, when someone bigger than you forces you to do things you wouldn't do for

$10,000, you better fucking believe you're a prisoner. He figured the best way to stay out of that kind of trouble was to become one of the people who wielded the law like a club, not one of the ones who cowered before it like whelps under the whip.

"Tell me in your own words what happened Chuck."

"I always stay at work a little late on Wednesdays. That's my bowling night. So instead of rushing home and then rushing to the bowling alley, I just take my stuff with me, put in an extra hour or so, and then get to the bowling alley. I eat while I'm there."

"You do this every week?"

"Well, during the league season. You know, sometimes I'll skip a week, something comes up with the kids and their school, or I'm achy or sick, or June has something she wants us to do together, you know. But most of the time I'm there."

"So what was different last night?"

"Nothing really. I was doing some stuff and Sharleen Sicarian stuck her head in my office and told me Felicia had missed her bus and needed a ride home. Before I could even answer, Sharleen was telling me how important it was that the girl get home so she could catch a plane. She was supposed to go visit her family or something."

"Why didn't Sicarian give her a lift?"

"I'm not sure."

"Didn't you ask?"

"No. She did say something about having too much to do, I think."

"You think?"

"Well, she always talked about having so much to do. I don't remember if that's what she said last night, or if she said it some other time."

"So, you didn't want to take the girl home?"

"Huh. Uh, no. I didn't want to be late for bowling."

"Did you tell your wife about this woman?"

"No."

"Why not? Were you afraid of what she would think?"

"Mr. Levy, Earl. What are you trying to say? I don't know how that can help me."

"If this thing gets to court, Chuck, I'm going to have to know everything. I know some of my questions might seem personal and not related to your case, but please answer all of them as completely as possible. Don't be embarrassed, your answers are protected by attorney-client privilege. And that includes June."

"I don't have anything to hide from my wife."

"We all have something we want to hide. I'm not saying that you would hurt anyone intentionally, but maybe you didn't mind taking the Tafoya girl home as much as you say. Maybe you found her attractive, or just interesting to talk to. So you figured it might not be so bad to spend a little time with a pretty, young woman. Find out what the young people are doing these days. Maybe find out if all those magazine articles about our promiscuous youth are true, maybe get lucky, get a little head or at least a good hand job?"

"No, no. How can you even suggest it? She was only a few years older than my own daughter..."

Gray's use of the past tense was not lost on Levy, "And your daughter's probably turning into quite a little woman now, and she probably has some cute, little friends..."

"That's disgusting. Who's side are you on? How is any of this going to help me?"

"I'm sorry, Chuck. I just have to know how you're going to react to what a prosecutor will certainly ask you. I didn't mean to upset you. It's just a method I use for getting the whole picture. I won't do it anymore.

"Please, tell me more about the girl. How old was she? How long had she worked with you? Do you know if she had any friends there, or about her family?"

"I'd guess she was in her early twenties." There was that past tense again, and something in Gray's eyes, he was staring at the floor but he wasn't seeing it. "She had long, straight, black hair, just past her waist, and she smiled a lot. She told me in the car that she was anxious about getting to the airport on time. She talked about her brothers and her mother. That's right, she was going to visit her mother in Mexico."

"Had you ever talked with her before last night?"

"No. She worked on the loading dock with a lot of other Hispanics. They talked in Spanish a lot, and I'd just kind of nod or say hello if we passed in a hall or I had to check out something on the dock or in the warehouse."

"So you saw Ms. Tafoya a lot."

"Oh no, no. I'm talking about all the people out there."

"Were there a lot of other young Hispanic woman on the docks and in the warehouse?"

"A half dozen or so. But I would say hello to guys too," Gray added hastily.

"Was Ms. Tafoya pretty?"

"I guess."

"What was she wearing the last time you saw her?"

"A red and black plaid flannel shirt and jeans. Oh, and she was wearing some fancy tennis shoes."

"Tennis shoes?"

"Whatever they call them these days. You know, sporty shoes like you see on television, Nike or Reeboks or something."

"You're sure?"

"Yeah, you can ask the people at work, someone must remember, why?"

"According to the report, the murdered girl was wearing a blue sweatshirt with jeans and Reeboks. Did you go into the house with her?"

"Of course not."

"And you're positive about the red and black flannel shirt?"

"Absolutely. Does this mean that I'm off the hook?"

"Well, assuming your memory is good, and she didn't do a fast change act in your car, there are two possible scenarios. One, the murdered girl is Felicia Tafoya, and she was raped and killed after she went into the house to change for the airport. Or, two, she isn't Felicia."

"Which proves that I'm innocent, right?"

"Well, if the murdered girl is Felicia, the evidence begins to turn away from you. But if it is another girl, you could still be implicated."

"I don't understand?"

"If there are others that can corroborate what you say Felicia was wearing, and she is the murdered girl, then she must have changed between the time you dropped her off and the time of the rape and murder. The prosecution will look at that as maybe someone else did it after you left, or that you're lying, or that you waited for her to come back out after she changed and then attacked her."

"That's ridiculous."

"Let's hope so. For them to begin to prove that, they would have to find someone who saw you parked and waiting. On the other hand, if the body isn't Tafoya's, the prosecution will suggest that you were turned on by the Tafoya girl but were too smart to rape and murder her, knowing that people would make the connection, so you went and found another victim, one you thought you couldn't be tied to."

"So, either way, they're going to come after me?"

"We don't know that for a fact. What happened when you got to the bowling alley? You must have a lot of friends there. Did you talk with anyone?"

"I talked to lots of people."

"No. I meant did you tell anyone there about having given the Tafoya girl a ride home?"

"No. Not specifically."

"What did you tell them, specifically? I mean, you were late, right? So what did you tell them?"

Gray was looking at the floor again. "I told them I had been working on a report that had to get done."

"Who's your best friend on your bowling team?"

"Pete."

"What did you tell him?"

"The same thing."

"What were you hiding?" Levy asked as gently as a robin landing in a tree.

"She was pretty. And sexy."

"It's all right, Chuck. No one else is going to find out about how you felt, not even Pete and June. It's natural, okay?"

"Okay."

"One more question. Why didn't you cooperate with the police?"

"I was scared. I was scared that June would find out about me taking the girl home. About, well what I just told you."

"Well, she knows about the girl now."

"Yeah."

Chapter 12

"Yes, Sharleen," Bob Benton looked up from his desk and motioned his assistant in.

"I'm sorry to bother you Bob. I just got off the phone with Lieutenant Norman."

"Did he have news about Chuck?"

"Well yes and no. I told him what I found out. He seemed very interested about the sexual harassments. He asked me to talk to the dock workers, find out if Chuck spends a lot of time out there, if he ever touched any of the girls there."

"It sounds like he still believes Chuck is the murderer?"

"Murderer and rapist."

"Yes, of course. But did the lieutenant tell you anything more about the case?"

"Two things. The police checked with Mexicana Airlines to find out if Felicia had been on the plane."

"Yes, what did they find out?" Benton was not appreciating Sicarian's born-again flare for the dramatic.

"Her seat was filled, that is, someone was sitting in it. But the plane was full to capacity. It had been overbooked, and there were over a half dozen stand-bys that got seats."

"So the seat might have been filled by someone else?"

"Right."

"But it might have been filled by Felicia Tafoya?"

"Yes. But that would only mean the woman who was raped and murdered was another Hispanic. Lieutenant Norman thinks it's plausible that Chuck was, uh, intrigued with Felicia…"

"You mean turned on sexually…"

"Uh, yes," Sicarian blushed. It was a subject she didn't like to acknowledge, though she had two children herself. And, during the past hour or so, she had even wondered if Chuck Gray ever noticed the derriere and breasts she did so much to keep firm.

"So what was Norman's point?"

"That, if Chuck was, you know, uh, turned on, that he might have left Felicia at her house and then gone and found another girl to rape and murder."

Benton wondered why his assistant had so much trouble saying sexually attracted, yet had no problem repeating rape and murder over and over again.

"So Chuck is screwed no matter who was on the plane?"

"There were three more things Lieutenant Norman mentioned." Benton cocked his head, signaling her to proceed. "The preliminary coroner's report indicates the woman died at about 6:15 last night, from strangulation."

"And?" Benton knew that he was going to have to hear her out.

"Well, that's the same time Chuck was in her neighborhood."

"What else did the lieutenant share with you?"

"Fluid samples show that the perpetrator was blood type O, the same as Chuck Gray."

"And millions of other men and women in this country."

"And there was evidence of HIV, but they don't know yet if it was from Feli … , I mean, the woman or the man."

"Oh my God," Benton said, not knowing why he should care if a murderer and rapist contracted AIDS, even if that person might be someone he'd known for almost 20 years.

* * *

"Mr. Levy? The desk sergeant told me you were here," Sergeant Ives said after the attorney acknowledged the officer's knock.

"Do you have something for me, detective?" the lawyer asked, knowing the only reason an officer would interrupt an attorney with his client was if there were some important news, or their time was up, which was unlikely.

"From the coroner's office," Ives said, handing a thin envelope to Levy.

"Thank you." From years of practice, Earl Levy learned to open and examine the contents of such envelopes without his client seeing the pages. He pulled out the three pages and held them directly in front of Chuck Gray's face while still holding onto the envelope. The papers created a formidable obstacle that Levy found defendants reluctant to try to read.

The maneuver this time was particularly effective as Gray just seemed to zone-out while his attorney examined the envelope's two 8x10, color glossies, and a photocopy of the coroner's preliminary report. The graphic depiction of the murdered girl would give a less experienced person nightmares for a month. Levy examined them dispassionately, looking as though he might critique the photographer. One full-color sheet taken at the scene of the crime showed a woman in a half fetal position on gravel. Her hands, elbows and knees were torn and bloody from the position in which she was forced to accept sex on top of the very same gravel where she died. In addition, her buttocks were bruised and there was dried blood about her anus.

The second 8x10 was a close-up of the woman's face and neck. Or what was left of her face. It too must have been pressed against the gravel as the assault from behind kept pushing and pulling her face along the gravel, breaking her nose and flaying her flesh, especially on her well-formed cheek bones, jaw and forehead. Her neck bore the purple imprints of the murderer's fingers.

Levy took a moment to look from the photos to Gray. His client sat still as a corpse, hands in his lap, head bent, eyes as vacant as the Bahamas during hurricane season. Could this man have done this? Levy wondered. Looking at the epitome of a Bob Crachet type of beneficence, the hardened attorney found it difficult to imagine. But his worldly experience taught him that fact is always more bizarre than fiction, and that in the dark reaches of the human psyche, even the most devoted mother might be capable of killing her own babies.

But, that was not really Levy's concern. His job was to defend his client, to pull out every stop, produce any kind of doubt in the mind of his jury, to let this man once again walk amongst the other Felicia Tafoyas of society. God, he hoped Gray was innocent.

Evoking all the principles of the late Evelyn Wood, Levy scanned the printed document included with the photos. Most of the information was boiler plate. Practiced eyes dove right down to the time of death like a hungry Doberman going for his Alpo: 6:15 p.m. Shit, just the wrong time. Exactly when Gray would have had opportunity. Means was a given: any male between the ages of fourteen and seventy probably had the means. With an unwilling victim and an average-sized erection it wouldn't take much to cause the bleeding and bruising that confirmed anal penetration. And a girl this size could be overcome by most men in the targeted age group, which probably accounted for 75 percent of the male population. And, judging by the dried semen on the girl's well-formed, brown buttocks, this was definitely a male.

The only avenue left was motive. Levy had to convince a jury that, unlike himself, Gray was a devoted husband and father. That there was nothing to impeach his credibility as a politically correct Ozzie Nelson. Which meant character witnesses from his friends, family, bowling team and fellow workers.

Scanning down the page further, Levy noted that semen and blood samples confirmed that the rapist had type O blood—he'd have to find out what blood type Gray was. Although, as the most common blood type in the world, the odds were against him getting lucky here. The victim's blood type was B.

Levy also noted on the report that there was vaginal penetration as well. And that, oh God, HIV was also present. So, whoever the misogynistic cretin was, one way or another, he probably already received his death sentence.

"What's it say?" Gray asked his attorney.

"Not much. Just the usual boiler-plate bullshit. By the way, do you know your blood type?"

"O. Is that what they found at the scene, type O?"

"I won't lie to you, Chuck. It was O. But you know that's the most common blood type."

"I thought it was A?"

"May as well be, there's only about four or five percentage points between them."

"You know your blood."

"I know my business. Don't panic. Right now the cops have much more to prove than you do. Their evidence is strictly circumstantial. They need reliable witnesses, people that may have seen you with the victim, who, by the way, still hasn't been identified."

"Why don't you let me see those pictures? I might be able to tell you if the girl is Felicia or not," Gray volunteered.

"Believe me, you don't want to see these pictures. And, it doesn't matter who the girl is. The fact is, the cops believe you raped and murdered a Hispanic female last night at about 6:15.

"You were in the neighborhood—that's opportunity. You are strong enough and big enough to have assaulted the woman—that's means. The only thing left is motive, and the cops are thinking that any man who can get a hard-on looking at a young girl in tight jeans and a sweat shirt, has motive.

"We need to discredit their charges. I want to talk with your friends, your co-workers and your wife. Who would you suggest at your job and among your friends?"

"The first person I'd like you to talk to is Pete Winslow. I bowl with him. June will get you the number. Also, Dave and Marty, they're on the team too. At work, shit, start with Bob Benton, my boss. I've been there almost 20 years. Also, Judy Marks, she's the head accountant. I've worked with her a long time too."

"Thanks. How're things here?"

"They suck. I think I was about to get raped or something in that holding cell. These people are animals."

"I understand. They don't relate to someone like you."

"What do you mean?"

"The Florsheim shoes, the twill pants, dress shirt, neatly barbered hair. It tells them you're establishment, you've made it in the world."

"But, I'm in here with them on a murder charge."

"They don't know what the charge is. They might think it's a white-collar crime. Something that netted you hundreds of thousands of dollars, for which you will serve a light sentence in a minimum-security prison, get out and still have the cash, plus interest.

"Or, worse, they might think you're a plant, or at least not to be relied on to share a confidence. So they banish you the only way they know how. Through intimidation."

"You know this stuff?"

"Unfortunately. It's too late today to get you arraigned, Chuck. But I'll get you into a smaller cell for the night. You'll be arraigned first thing tomorrow morning. Can you raise any bail money?"

"How much?"

"It's a very serious crime. But, it is a first offense, you don't have any other kind of record, you have a wife and kids, member of the community. I'd guess about $250,000."

"$250,000. I don't have that kind of money. Oh God."

"It's going to be all right Chuck," the attorney reached out a hand and patted Gray on his shoulder. "I'll get in touch with a bondsman and have him ready to put up a bond using your house as security."

"My house isn't worth that much. I don't have that kind of equity."

"It's not a home-equity loan, Chuck. I'll explain it all later. For now, just trust me."

"Sure, okay," he was relieved. For the first time since Sharleen Sicarian had walked into his office with the two policemen that morning, it seemed that something was finally going right. Someone was taking control, taking the pressure off him and making everything all right. If the attorney had told him to sign over his new car, quit his job and rob a bank so he wouldn't have to worry about any of this ever again, he would have done it with the confidence and devotion of a Bolshevik.

Chapter 13

True to his word, Levy got Chuck Gray into a cell with just one other criminal, a crack head who figured Gray for a narc and gave him a wide berth. The other man's physique had been so ravaged by the '90s version of opium that he posed no physical threat to Gray. However, an ongoing diatribe about the world, and specifically the police, kept Gray on edge.

"Fucking cops," the man would always begin his next speech. "Man, why can't they just leave you the fuck alone? You know. If I want to fuck up my body, man, that should be my business. What the fuck should they care for? They're just busting people to make the politicians look good. Man, this whole fucking war on drugs is just a fucking smoke screen. You know what I mean? They just don't want people to think about all the shit they do, you know, like fucking their little campaign workers, and getting tax-free stuff done for their rich friends..."

Gray wished for silence. The peace and quiet of a corner where he could curl up with a good book. But there were no books. There was no television, magazines, newspapers, radios or even a mail-order catalog. All they had in their cell were two bunk beds that came out from the wall, another stainless steel, seatless toilet, a small table and a chair. And this babbling idiot was in the chair when Gray was delivered. His laments wearing long as a religion and thin as a belief.

Gray's only reprieve would come at dinnertime. Then he would get a little quiet as his cellmate slowly picked at luke-warm meatloaf served alongside green beans the color of camouflage and squishy mashed potatoes. Gray found he could stomach a little of the evening's repast by mixing it all together and dousing it liberally with salt, pepper and catsup. His only other sauce being the hunger that came from having not ingested anything since his 10 a.m. latte.

* * *

In jails, meals are served early. This is so clean up and other chores can be completed at a reasonable time to let correctional institution employees go home and enjoy some time with their families, friends or what-have-you. On the outside, as prisoners are cleaning up dishes and washing down mess halls, those with freedom are just getting ready for their evening. Happy housewives are setting tables, young professionals are powering up microwaves, the important, the wealthy and the pretenders are picking outfits from their wardrobes to wear to posh night spots, hoping to be spotted by anything but the cuisine.

Still others have business and affairs to discuss over dinner, with the government sporting half the tab—if their accountants were any good. In this last category were Earl Levy and June Gray.

Acting more proper than his thoughts, the attorney had his secretary contact the wife of his client to arrange a meeting to discuss the case at a well-established eatery. An up-and-coming hot spot would not do for a professional appointment, and the restaurant of a fine hotel might seem too suggestive—Levy had even told his secretary to leave open the option of an early morning meeting in his office. No, none of those would suit the occasion. Only the formal dark burl booths of a venerated old restaurant would provide the proper ambiance of a consultation, and the slightest suggestion of a tryst.

Like many others this Thursday evening, June Gray examined her wardrobe for the perfect image. But, all the colors fuzzed out into soft pastels from a sheen of tears that blurred her vision like Vaseline on a camera lens. She had been home for hours. It was pointless to go back to the school after she saw her husband in jail. An already mild-mannered person, he had been reduced to a quivering mass. Smelling of urine, his pants soiled, what was June to think, to feel? She knew she hadn't married a charismatic leader, or even a man who would make his mark as a department head in a major company. But Chuck Gray had always been able to hold his head up. He earned an honest living. He cared for his family and others. He had dignity and pride. He was someone other than the man she saw this afternoon; especially in contrast to the Armani-suited, peacock, Earl Levy.

She knew she should have waited for Mr. Levy after she left the conference room at the precinct. However, a different pilot took over the seat of rationality in her and she just kept going; from the conference room to the reception area, out the doors and over to her Nissan Sentra. Her keys were already in her hand and she just slid behind the wheel and took off toward the middle school where she taught. She was within sight of the school when the auto-pilot got hit up the side of the head and parachuted out in favor of her consciousness. The rest of the afternoon flashed in front of her eyes, June Gray, convict's wife, standing up in front of her classes, smelling of urine, her dress soiled. Had she peed on herself too, or did she get the stain and the smell from Chuck? She had no idea.

Wheeling the car around, she headed for home, pulled into the garage and entered through the laundry room. It was far enough. As the automatic garage door groaned to a close, she stripped off her foul-smelling outfit and stuffed every article into the washer, regardless of color, fabric or washing instructions. Grabbing up her bag and shoes, she walked buck naked up to her room and the comfort of a hot shower. She washed and scrubbed like a rape victim. Soap lathered up like snow drifts on her genitals, her breasts and her hair.

Poor Chuck, she thought as she rinsed and lathered up a second time—was that for him? Her harmless husband now locked up with God-only-knew-who. And what would happen to him? Did men get raped in local jails, or was that only in prisons? Shit, that's like asking if people only die in hospitals.

Rinsing for the second time she knew there was nothing she could do for him. If only he had told her where he had been last night. It would look a lot better. And, why didn't he say anything? Was he attracted to that woman he took home? Had he seen her before? Was it possible he did rape and murder her? Maybe they had been lovers every week on bowling night, and she wanted to break it off, and he got crazy. Oh no. It couldn't be. Not Chuck. He would never do anything like that to another human being. But, maybe it was an accident? After all, June Gray didn't know how the woman died. Maybe she fell and hit her head, long after Chuck had left, long after he had dropped her off at her house for the first and only time ever, and she slipped on something and hit her head and the cops think she was struck? Maybe that's what happened?

The soap opera of her mind continued relentlessly; after all, he did come home and make love to her last night. Was that something someone would do if he had just raped and murdered a woman and then bowled three games? That's like saying that people only die in hospitals.

Wishing she could change the channel in her brain to a comedy or a musical. Christ, even a western or a football game, any fucking thing except the alternating reality and ghastly visions that played against her clamped, damp eyelids as she buried her face in the pillows that lined the head of their bed.

She had no idea how long she had been lying nude on the firm, king-sized bed when the phone rang. "Hello," she said as empty as a torn grocery sack.

"Mrs. Gray?" a professionally polite voice asked.

"Yes?"

"I hope I'm not disturbing you, this is Apricot Jones at Earl Levy's office."

"I'm sorry, did you say Apricot Jones?"

"Yes. I know it's an unusual name. It comes from a craving my mother had when she was pregnant."

June smiled despite herself. Maybe that's why Earl Levy hired her. "Yes Ms. Jones?"

"Mr. Levy asked me to call and find out how you're doing?"

"Under the circumstances, pretty shitty. I'm sorry dear. It was kind of you…and him. I'm just sort of numb."

"Is there anything we can do for you Mrs. Gray?"

"Nothing more than you're already doing, thank you."

"Mr. Levy also wants to know if you would be up to meeting with him to discuss your husband's case. He's booked through the afternoon, but he suggested getting together for dinner, or first thing in the morning. Whichever is more convenient?"

June Gray's first inclination was to jump at the dinner invitation. Then she felt guilty. Her husband in jail, maybe in trouble there, and she out dining with handsome Earl Levy. A "tomorrow morning will be best" was coalescing in her mind when she realized that where she was that night had no bearing on her husband's well being behind bars. And, she rationalized, the sooner she and the lawyer talked, the sooner they could do something for Chuck. "This evening will be fine."

"Mr. Levy will pick you up at seven. Is that all right?"

"Yes, that will be fine," her voice trailed off like a drop of water on a Gortex boot.

Chapter 14

Work throughout the paper goods warehouse proceeded as usual. The main event of the day, the arrest of Chuck Gray, comptroller, in the late morning had been thoroughly absorbed and debated by the time the union-imposed three o'clock break arrived.

Of course, there were still whispers and conjecture about Gray. "You know Sylvia," Hilda Rodriguez said as she stretched two-inch wide Scotch tape around a small order of second sheets and envelopes for a late pick up, "that Gray guy sure spent a lot of time down here in the warehouse. Maybe he didn't get enough at home, eh?"

"I don't know Hilda," her co-worker answered, "he seemed pretty nice. You know, one time I slipped and was about to fall on my butt. He was nearby and grabbed me. His hand touched my breast as he caught me, boy was he embarrassed when he realized it."

And later, in the break room, Hilda was talking with Mary and repeated the story, "So, Sylvia told me that Gray guy once grabbed her boob by accident, and was really embarrassed when they both noticed it."

"Uh, huh," Mary was telling Jennifer as they walked down the hall from the break room, past Sharleen Sicarian, to the warehouse. "He tried to feel her up once and got really upset when she caught him."

The overheard conversation reminded the administrative assistant that she wanted to drop in on the accounting department, just to be sure everything was running smoothly in Gray's absence. She made a mental note of Jennifer Reynold's comment and proceeded to Gray's office where she jotted the gist of the conversation down on a scratch pad, removed the sheet and stuck it in the pocket of her suit jacket. She also casually flipped a few pages of Gray's calendar, going back in time and trying to decipher cryptic entries such as the four o'clock notation on the 17th, "Blondie" which might be interpreted as an afternoon tryst, a note about Helen, the attractive young natural blonde in the bookkeeping bullpen—visible through the usually open door of Gray's office, a sexist commentary about a meeting with Sicarian—a semi-natural blonde herself (she would have to cross-check her calendar). Or, unbeknownst to Sicarian, it might be a reminder to attend the rehearsal of a play his daughter was in at school—a send-up of the nearly-forgotten series of movies that ran from 1938 to 1950.

Drifting in from the bullpen came the same blonde voice of Helen MacGaw as she wheeled her chair around toward the filing cabinet, and Gray's doorway, talking on the phone, "Uh huh. Yeah, but the really kinky thing was that he wanted to keep the panties," the beginning and end of the conversation were obscured by her turning her back from the doorway. Sicarian semi-consciously circled the entry on Gray's calendar with the pen she had in her hand. She also made a mental note to talk with Ms. MacGaw about making personal calls on company time.

"If any of you have any questions while Mr. Gray and Ms. Marks are out," Sicarian addressed the accounting bullpen, "you may direct them to me." She interpreted the succeeding silence as an affirmation that everything was under control, and walked back to her office.

Even before she reached her door, the decision had been made to drop in on Bob Benton. The CEO was standing by a window when she entered. "Bob, I've been doing a little snooping, and I think we really do have a situation here," she took a step or two into the room, but had left the door ajar.

"I understand, Sharleen, I had hoped that the police would consider this episode with Chuck Gray an unfortunate mistake, and that he would be back here by now."

"It may go further than just his arrest," she paused waiting for her boss, but he didn't say anything. A silence that was noted by Clarice, the secretary whose desk was right outside Benton's door.

"It appears that Chuck had fondled one of the girls in the warehouse, and might have made some lewd remarks to a woman in the accounting department."

"How come we didn't hear about this before?"

"I think our Hispanic workers don't understand that they need to report incidents like this. Maybe they're afraid that if they say something about the white workers it will hurt them."

"What about the girl in accounting, is she Hispanic too?"

"No, but she might feel that talking about it would jeopardize her job, since accounting reports directly to Chuck. Or, they might be having an affair."

"But I thought you said he had made a lewd remark to her?"

"It's a comment that I would consider lewd. But she may have different values."

"Do you think I should call Lieutenant Norman and tell him about these other incidents?"

"Chuck's in enough trouble already. Perhaps you should wait."

"Okay. Whatever you say," she turned and left, reprimanding herself for having left the door ajar. But observing with gratification that Clarice still had her dictation head phones on and was typing away at her computer keyboard. Satisfied she had maintained company security, Sharleen walked to her office, made sure the door was closed and began entering the information she had about Chuck Gray into a password-protected file on her computer, just in case.

Clarice's head phone set did indeed obscure hearing in her left ear, the one that would be seen by someone coming out of Bob Benton's office. However, since the right ear piece was snuggled up against the black springy hair next to her right ear, and since the dictation machine was off anyway, she heard practically every word spoken in the boss's office, while she let her hands gently rest on the keyboard of her computer, ready to begin typing anything at a moment's notice.

"Girl, it's true. This guy's been groping women around here for years," Clarice was on the phone to her friend in purchasing. "You' all just lucky he didn't come in there all the time like he did with the girls in the warehouse, and the ones working for him in accounting … You bet I know it. I heard ol' Sharleen talking to Bob about it. Girl, he had been touching women and talking trash for a long time. I feel bad for that Felicia Tafoya. And, you know ol' Sharleen's not going to sleep well for a while. Why she practically shoved that girl in that perv's car. She might as well have told him to go fuck her and kill her. Uh huh, that's gotta be a lot to have on your conscience. We better be real cool for awhile around ol' Sharleen, she going to be on the rag about this for a long time … You bet, I wouldn't want to have that on my conscience … Yes ma'am, I'll take care of that right away," Clarice's entire tone and speech turned on a dime as Bob Benton emerged from his office.

"Clarice, I've got an appointment and probably won't be back until after five. Just take messages and I'll take care of them when I get back or tomorrow morning," Benton said, hardly breaking his stride.

* * *

"Julian," Clarice's friend in purchasing said to her co-worker. "You know that guy the cops busted this morning?"

"Mr. Gray?" Julian replied.

"Yeah, him," and she filled in the details.

"That sonofabitch," Julian said when Clarice's friend was through, "they ought to cut off his nuts."

Chapter 15

June Gray said goodbye to Apricot Jones and hung up the phone. Realizing she was still naked, she felt suddenly embarrassed, as if she should have been dressed when she was talking to her husband's lawyer's secretary. She also became aware of her erect nipples and decided it must be from the cold, even though the temperature in the house was rarely lower than 68 degrees.

Putting on a robe, June went back downstairs to the kitchen where the answering machine was. As she anticipated, there was a message from her school wanting to know if she would be in to teach tomorrow. There was a message from her son Zane, letting her know he was going over to his friend Paul's after school to shoot some hoops and "stuff."

Since it was nearing five, she opted to wait until tomorrow morning to call the school. She wasn't sure if she would be able to muster the energy it would take to face her colleagues, much less her class, after they heard the evening news, or got word about Chuck from the grapevine—which was bound to be worse. June also wondered why she hadn't heard from her daughter, Evelyn. She was supposed to be giving her speech for president of the debate club today. Maybe she hadn't done well and was drowning her sorrows with a Coke and fries at Mickey D's.

Just then the front door opened and June identified the footsteps as a pair of black leather, low-heeled pumps she bought Evelyn at the mall a few months ago. Actually, she identified the footsteps as being female, and she remembered Evelyn begging this morning to let her wear the fancy shoes to school so she would look nice, and taller, when she was giving her speech in front of the debate club.

As Evelyn entered the kitchen June was smiling for the first time since she had been summoned to the principal's office and found out that Evelyn's father had been arrested. June was thinking about her little girl, the fuss about the black pumps and how she wanted to look taller when she gave her speech. June knew she would remember that precious moment forever—except it fled from her mind like a campaign promise on election day the moment her daughter came into view. She looked bigger all right, like her breasts were going to pop right over the top of the little lace bra that strained against her translucent blouse. Not only had the little slut worn the sexy lace push-up bra June begrudgingly let her buy, but she had obviously stuffed it full of tissue to achieve the cleavage that was hardly hidden behind the white rayon blouse.

Evelyn's eyes followed June's gaze down to her chest, in her surprise at finding her mother home so early, Evelyn had forgotten all about her "ace-in-the-hole" to win the election. "Mom, I can explain," Evelyn tried to head off the verbal attack that the seismograph of June Gray's face registered. "My bras get all sweaty in gym class. And I didn't want to wear a sweaty old bra to give my speech, and this was the only clean one I had, so I grabbed it. Just in case, you know? And the other one did get all sweaty, so I changed."

June just stood there, her anger about her daughter's deceit and lies blending like a river of magma with her husband's improprieties and lies to form a rampaging lava flow that would rip through her like Mt. St. Helens. Surprisingly to both mother and daughter, when June finally did open her mouth, she did not shout. In a voice as even and unrelenting as the Bonneville salt flats she said, "Young lady, I am older, smarter and more experienced than you. I know that when a girl tries to win friends, favors or an election by stuffing her bra with tissue, she loses. Maybe not the election, but certainly a portion of her self-esteem. By putting your physical attributes ahead of your personal abilities you do an injustice to both. There is no amount of Kleenex you can stuff into your mind or soul that will give you what you need to respect yourself and have others love you for who you are."

It was Evelyn's turn to stand dumbfounded. Tears ran from unblinking eyes down magenta cheeks, trailing alongside tight blue veins in her neck and finally wending their way down into the shadowy cleavage for which she worked so hard, and paid so dearly. Turning on one of her short stacked heels, the young woman ran from the kitchen up to her bedroom.

Like any good mother, June was torn. She had vented her rage, expiating her frustration and filling the room with righteous indignation. But in her bosom she ached. Ached for her daughter and the grief she now bore. And for what? For showing her womanhood? Was it Evelyn's fault that even in this age of supposed equality, girls were still getting the message that the size of their breasts counted for more than the measure of their abilities?

It isn't just the boys, either. Magazines from *Seventeen* to *Cosmo*—magazines targeted to women of various ages—touted the desirability of a D-cup décolletage. And well-formed tushes, flat abs and firm legs. How can women compete? Sure, they admire a handsome man who's in shape. But that attraction wears thin quickly. Besides, clothing covers up almost everything a man might have to offer. But with women, they're out there, preceding them into a room, resting comfortably atop a table, desk or a pair of folded arms like twin offerings to the Gods. June Gray knew; even in her junior high school class the little boys stared at her breasts, their little trousers sometimes filling up with tumescent little dicks.

Yes she was torn. She knew it wasn't Evelyn's invention to wear the sexiest bra she owned, or to stuff it with tissues. Shit, it wasn't as if June herself didn't dress to the nines for the right occasion. It wasn't as if she didn't feel a little pride when a man had to force his attention from her breasts to her face. It wasn't as if she hadn't contemplated wearing the black lace C-cup version of Evelyn's little indiscretion to her dinner with Earl Levy that night —though she had no need to assist nature with paper products.

June was also torn because she wanted to go and comfort Evelyn. To hold her and let her know that what she did wasn't so bad. That it was just inappropriate. And that it is a parent's job to point these things out to their children, to guide them and let them know what kind of an impression they give a thoroughly-jaded society through their actions. June also knew she had to tell Evelyn that her father was in jail. But together, mother and daughter had blown it. They would both have to go to their separate corners to lick their wounds before they could broach any more touchy subjects.

With this sad thought in her mind, and the dread of having to tell her teenage daughter about something heinous, about something that she prayed with all her soul wasn't true, June ascended the stairway back to her bedroom. Evelyn's escapade made June rethink her attire for the evening. Out from her lingerie drawer came a bra that offered nearly complete coverage. Like the one she had been contemplating, it was black lace, but under a smart, business-like green silk blouse, one could hardly think of it as sexy. She slipped into a pair of her standard, cotton bikini panties, pulled on black panty hose and was shimmying into a straight black skirt when Evelyn appeared at the partially open door and gave a little knock.

"Hi, honey," June said to her contrite daughter.

"Mom, I'm…"

"It's okay honey. I just hope you realize what you did was wrong. Not just wearing something inappropriate for all the wrong reasons, but for lying. Don't forget, I was your age once, and things weren't as good for women then as they are now. And, if young women like you aren't careful how you act, they may very well slip back to the way they were. It's okay to look pretty, even sexy at the right time, just don't abuse it."

"I understand, Mom," Evelyn said to the floor. She had changed into baggy jeans and a sweatshirt. It was hard for June to tell whether or not she was still wearing the formidable lingerie under the sweatshirt, but judging by her daughter's demeanor, and the softness of her form, it was her educated guess that the offending garment was tucked away in a dresser drawer.

"There's something else I have to tell you, dear," June said, tucking her blouse into the skirt before sitting down on her bed and patting the spot next to her. Evelyn came over and sat next to her mom like a trained cocker spaniel.

"Something's wrong, isn't it?"

"What makes you ask?"

"You're never home this early. Is Dad okay? Did something happen to Zane?"

"They're both all right, that is, there hasn't been an accident or anything."

"But there is something wrong?"

"Yes, dear. I don't even know how to tell you this. It… I mean… Oh damnit," June finally broke through the barrier and, as tears began to trace their way from her eyes to the creases by her nose she just blurted out, "Your father's been arrested."

"What? Dad? That can't be. It's some kind of a mistake. How can that be?"

"I know, I know dear. It must be a mistake. Your father is so kind and gentle, it has to be a mistake."

"What happened? Why?" Evelyn's confusion was expressed with tears like her mother's.

"Last night, a girl was attacked. Your father's car was seen in the area. But that doesn't mean he was involved."

"Was she raped?" Evelyn's voice flattened out enough to creep under a door.

"Yes."

"Can't she identify who did it?"

"I'm afraid not."

"She's dead?" Evelyn's tears stopped, behind her eyes was a screen of darkness like the backside of a theater screen, a movie playing vividly on the other side to an audience of one.

"Yes."

"It couldn't have been Dad. He doesn't even hit me when I'm bad. He couldn't do it, he doesn't have the…"

"You were going to say 'the nerve,' or 'the balls'? Don't look so shocked Evie, your generation didn't invent that phrase. More importantly, you must understand that real men don't have to prove themselves by hitting women. It takes more balls to understand and contain your anger or hurt than to lash out at someone." June listened closely to herself as she lectured Evelyn, the words were important to her. She wanted to believe them, she didn't want to think of the world's John Wayne Gaseys and Ted Bundys, and she certainly didn't want to expose her daughter to thoughts about Jekyll and Hyde personalities, repressed violent tendencies or suppressed sexual drives.

"Are you getting dressed to visit Dad?" Evelyn asked.

"Uh, no. I have a meeting with his lawyer, to discuss what we can do. I saw him this afternoon, and he's doing okay. Of course," June began to fabricate a more palatable scenario for her daughter, "he's upset about being arrested, and very sad about what happened to the girl, even though he has no idea who she is. He looked good and was being strong. The police have him in a cell by himself so he doesn't have to be around hardened criminals. He told me to send you and Zane his love. Thinking about you gives him strength. He promises he'll be home tomorrow, and wanted you to know especially that he will be in the audience on opening night to see you in 'Blondie.'"

June was relieved to see the tears begin to roll down Evelyn's cheeks again. She had gotten through to her. She pulled Evelyn close. As the child calmed down in the secure embrace of her mother, June just hoped she could convince herself of half of what she had just said.

And then there was Zane. She couldn't leave the house without talking to him. But she wasn't sure what time he would be home. On a normal week day, he was supposed to be in by six, and he usually made it within fifteen minutes. It was already a little past, so June thought she better call his friend Paul's house and tell him to come home right away, if he hadn't already left. She still had to put some dinner on the table for the kids, they could clean up afterwards, and, she figured, given the circumstances, they were responsible enough to do their homework.

"Evie, honey, I'm going to call Paul's house and find out if Zane is still there. Would you start some pasta boiling and I'll fix you both a salad and some Prego, will that be okay for dinner?"

"I'm not very hungry, Mom."

"I understand, dear. But you have to eat something. Not eating won't help your father, and it won't help you either. We'll just put something together quick, and you just eat what you want. I'm sure your brother will finish whatever is left, all right?"

"Okay."

Once Evelyn was out of the bedroom, June called over to Paul's home. It was only a few blocks away. Though the Grays and Paul's folks, the Kirchners, weren't close, they had sat together at little league games, said hello at PTA meetings and were on a first name basis. "Hello, Linda? This is June Gray. Is Zane still there?"

"Oh June. Uh, yes, I'll call him to the phone." She knew. godamnit, she knew. It must be on the television. Shit, why hadn't she thought to turn on the goddamn television before she called? What if Zane already knew? She wouldn't be able to talk with him like she talked to Evelyn.

"Mom?" the deepening masculine voice of her son was on the phone.

"Hello dear. I would like you to come home now. I need to talk to you," she hoped he would just agree without asking any questions.

"About Dad? I already know. He raped and murdered a woman last night. And then he came home and slept in our house. How can you want me to come back to that house?"

"Zane. Zane. Your father has been accused of those things. But you don't really think he could do anything like that, do you? Everyone likes your father, he's good to you and your sister, he's never lifted a hand to anyone in this family—to anyone. Zane, in your heart you know it's a mistake. Please Zane, please come home. Your father's in jail for the night. I have to meet with his lawyer in half an hour. I need to have you here for your sister. I need to have you here for me. Please Zane, please come home, I need you."

"I'm sorry, Mom. Yeah, I'll be there in ten minutes." Zane acquiesced to his mother's entreaties. He gathered up his jacket and backpack, noticed their relief as he said goodbye to the Kirchners, and headed out the door.

As Zane walked toward his home, he reflected on what June told him about his father. How everyone liked him. How mild mannered he was. But Zane was a man now himself. He understood men's needs and urges a lot better than his mother, he thought. How could she know what it was like to get a hard-on when you see a nice set of boobs? He didn't understand it himself. He just knew about that throbbing appendage in his pants that could shoot a stream of semen more than a foot when properly stimulated by himself with the visual assistance of the Playmate of the Month, a model in Victoria's Secret, some television cleavage, a girl in his class, a friend of his little sister. Shit, even by his little sister with her growing titties that he could catch a peek of as she got out of the shower or into her pajamas. Hell, his penis was already responding to all the "women" in his life, even as he walked home.

Chapter 16

Then Zane began to think of his father in jail. The boy's erection deflated amid mental images of television-stereotype, greasy biker types circling about the cell like vultures. He pictured his father in the middle of this circle; a virgin kneeling before demonic priests. These leather-armored priests had their own religion, the religion of dominance. It didn't matter if it was a man or woman pleading for mercy, their zeal was fed by fear. The fact that one or more of them might ram their cock up his father's ass, or any other orifice in the universe, was not to sate a sexual urge, it was to create terror.

Zane knew about this and other aberrant behavior from watching the nightly news programs that proliferate the television channels on the far edge of prime time. It made some sense to him, although the thought of him sliding his member into a protesting woman's front, face or backside brought a certain erotic thrill to his mind, even as it conflicted with his feelings about men who did such things. Maybe he *was* like his father, he thought as he walked the last block to his house.

According to news reports about his father and the murdered woman, she had been sodomized by her attacker. Sodomized, meaning any sex act except penal/vaginal intercourse. Ergo, ass fucking, face fucking, jerking off, being jerked off, having a guy jerk you off, doing it with a piece of liver like in *Portnoy's Complaint*—interesting how many bad ways there are to have sex, and how few right ways. Of course, he knew the news people weren't talking about any kind of hand job. His father, no, he quickly corrected himself, whoever the animal was that did this thing either forced his dick up the girl's ass or down her throat, probably in addition to the standard, sanctified fuck.

Zane couldn't believe that his father would do such a thing. But then, who would believe that Zane would sneak peeks at his sister and her friends? At his age, he thought that no one suspected.

"Thank you for coming home right away Zane," June Gray said to her son as he entered the kitchen. "I'm making spaghetti and a salad for you and your sister. Is there anything else I can get you before I leave?"

"Naw."

"You two help each other out, okay? I want you to clean up the kitchen when you finish. Talk to each other if it will help, but don't forget to do your homework. I'll try to get home early if you need to talk more.

"I'm sure this is all a big mistake. Maybe the lawyer can get your dad out tonight, and we'll come home together. Wouldn't that be nice?" she was almost living up to her perky namesake.

"That would be great mom," Zane answered instinctively, knowing from his television viewing that his father wouldn't be arraigned until morning.

"Gee, that would be wonderful," Evelyn chimed in, ignorant of her brother's viewing habits.

"Okay then, I'll see what we can do," June answered, taking their support to heart. "I heard a car pull up, that must be Mr. Levy."

She was out in the hall and slipping into a jacket that matched her skirt by the time the doorbell rang. She peered through the peephole and saw Earl Levy in an expensive, dark suit, a pink dress shirt complemented beautifully by a red silk tie and matching handkerchief.

June opened the door just a sliver and slipped out like a bad pun at a funeral to avoid having her children catch a glimpse of the handsome attorney. "Hi."

"Hi. Is everything okay? I mean, under the circumstances?"

"Yes. I've talked with the kids. Made them some dinner. I think they'll be all right," she told him as he escorted her to his BMW and held the door for her.

"Is continental all right? I thought we might go to the Normandy."

"I'm not very hungry, but I'm sure they'll have a salad or something," she felt guilty and confused. What was Chuck having for dinner? She was sure the company wasn't as pleasant. And whatever the ambiance, it wouldn't even compare to that of the kitchen help at the Normandy. Why was she going out with lawyer Levy anyway? What could they accomplish at a restaurant that they couldn't talk about on the phone, or in his office tomorrow morning?

As the attorney pulled the car from the curb she caught his profile in the oncoming headlights and remembered that the secretary with the funny name had opened the door to a morning meeting. But June had declined. She didn't want to think it was because of handsome features, she didn't want to think there was any attraction. Oh, how convenient. She knew where her husband was, she knew she had the whole night if she wanted it, she knew the attorney was attracted to her.

"I'm sorry, Earl. I don't think this is such a good idea."

"The restaurant or the meeting?" his voice was soft and full of understanding.

"Both. I mean, nothing personal, you seem like a wonderful man, but with Chuck in jail, and my kids at home, I just don't think I should be having dinner at a fancy restaurant with you."

"I understand. And I hope I didn't give you the wrong impression. I do need to talk to you about your husband, get some background information to prepare briefs and motions. But that can wait. We can meet at my office in the morning.

"I must admit that I was looking forward to this evening though. I don't often mix business with pleasure. But there is something about you that is so very rare. The way your eyes sparkle with intelligence, the dignified way you carry yourself. Well, besides being selfish by wanting to spend time with you, I thought getting you away from the events of the day might be relaxing for you.

"Are you sure you won't reconsider? We both need to eat. And we really do have to discuss your husband's case. It's only seven-something, I can have you back home by nine, nine-thirty, the latest. It would be a shame to hang up such a handsome suit and beautiful blouse without ever exposing them to the risk of a salad dressing stain."

She smiled despite herself. "I suppose arguing with a professional would be a waste of time?"

"Is that a yes?"

"Was there ever any doubt?" she asked.

"What do you mean?"

"Well, you kept on driving toward the restaurant."

"How do you know I wasn't just looking for a place to turn around?"

"I'm glad you didn't phrase that as a demonstrative statement, lying wouldn't become you."

"Touché."

* * *

It seemed as though her mother had only been gone a few minutes when the phone rang. Evelyn leaped for the instrument in typical teenage fashion. "Hello."

"May I please speak with Evelyn?"

"This is she," the young woman answered, taking the cordless phone into the living room where she hoped her brother wouldn't be able to eavesdrop.

"This is Mark Pierce, from the debate club." She tried in vain to conjure a picture of Mark Pierce. The problem, of course, was that she didn't pay much attention to the boys in the debate club. They were all nerds in white shirts with pocket protectors, as far as she was concerned. She wouldn't be in the club at all, except that it looked good on her academic record.

"Oh, yes, Mark. How are you?" she still had no idea who she was talking to, but she still wanted to win the presidency of the club, and to be rude now would be to lose what sounded like a sure vote. If he had any friends, there might even be more than one vote at stake.

"I'm fine. I wasn't sure you knew who I was. I liked your speech today."

"Of course I know who you are," she lied. "You were wearing a really nice white shirt today."

"Oh, you noticed. Well, I just wanted to call and tell you that I think you're really cool. I'm going to vote for you and get my friends to vote for you too."

"That's really nice of you Mark."

"And, I was wondering if I could come over tonight. To talk about the debate club and stuff."

"Well, I have homework that I have to do. It's in geometry. It will probably take me a long time, geometry's not my best subject," she said, trying to avoid spending any time at all with someone that had the sex appeal of toenail clippings.

"Wow, geometry's my best subject, I can come over and help you. You'll be done in no time."

"I really appreciate that, Mark, but uh, my mom wants me to do it myself. She's a teacher, and she says I'll learn it better if I have to do it myself."

"She's right, of course. But I tutor kids in geometry. I won't just do your homework, I'll help you learn it." Evelyn's ruse wasn't working. To fence further with this Mark Pierce would be to let on that she wasn't interested, which could lead to the loss of important votes.

"That's nice of you to offer Mark. Why don't you come by in about a half hour? Do you know where I live?"

"Uh, huh. I'll see you then." When he hung up she wondered how he knew where she lived, and where he got her phone number. He could have looked it up online, but it was listed under her parents' names. She would have to remember to ask him when he arrived.

* * *

As his sister talked on the phone in the living room, Zane set the table and drained the spaghetti. He waited patiently for his younger sister to finish her conversation and come to the table. He hoped she wouldn't take too long, he didn't want the pasta to get cold. He was rewarded with her quick return to the kitchen.

"Hey, thanks for taking the pasta off the stove," Evelyn said when she got back. "I guess home ec pays off."

"Sure. Why don't you take what you want first?" His offer was only half magnanimous, he was counting on her taking a much smaller portion and leaving the rest for him.

"Yeah, then you can have the rest," Evelyn understood the appetite of teenage boys, or at least, she thought she did.

"What do you think about this business with Dad?" Zane asked.

"It must be a mistake," Evelyn answered as she reconsidered her portion of pasta and put some back in the colander. "Dad couldn't do anything like that to someone. Shit. He's never even spanked us."

"Maybe not you. But he once hit me with his belt when I got suspended from school for cheating on a test."

"Like you didn't deserve it."

"I didn't say that. It's just that, maybe, given the right circumstances he can do something like that."

"Like what kind of circumstances?" Evelyn asked as Zane joined her at the table with all the pasta and sauce that was left.

"I don't know. Maybe if we were in Nazi Germany?"

"Do you really think so? I think he would just pray that everything would get better."

"What if he were really pissed off, or he really wanted something badly?" Zane asked.

"Like what? To fuck someone else besides mom?"

"Evelyn."

"Don't you think they do it, Zane?"

"Well, of course. We're here. But they're, well, you know…"

"They still do it, goofball. People always do it. Once they start, they never stop. Maybe they slow down, but they never stop. And I don't think they ever stop thinking about it or wondering how it might be with someone else."

"You think Mom and Dad go around all day fantasizing about other people? You're crazy. People don't do that after they've grown up."

"Oh, grow up yourself, Zane. Why do you think there are all those men's magazines, and the ones for women get into the same stuff, just differently. You should read some of the women's magazines, if you really want to *know* what is going on, instead of just getting off on the pictures in those other magazines.

"There are studies that say men and women think about sex a lot more than you might expect. They don't think about it with everyone they meet. They don't do anything about it most of the time, but they think about it a lot."

"I read about guys that think about sex as much as every eight seconds. Maybe that's why there's so many sexual harassment suits."

"Maybe it's because women think guys think about sex every eight seconds that there are so many suits. Every eight seconds they think the guy in the room with them is thinking about sex, so they feel harassed."

"You're so full of shit."

"Does that mean you think Dad could have done it?" Zane asked.

"I think that he might have had thoughts about some girl. But I don't think he could have done something like that." Her assessment of the situation made her feel better, and she continued with conviction, "I'm sure it is some kind of mistake and they'll be letting him out of jail very soon."

"I hope you're right," Zane answered, his television savvy telling him that not every innocent man goes free.

* * *

True to his word again, Earl Levy kept the dinner on a platonic/business level. While he didn't take any notes, his questions were well organized, concise and relevant. Of course, that did not preclude some small talk and intimate probing. By 10:00, when the couple slid back into Earl Levy's BMW, June felt comfortably known to the talented mouthpiece.

"I can have you home by 10:15. Or we can go back to my place for a nightcap?" Levy ventured.

Chapter 17

It was back about the time Earl Levy poured June Gray her first glass of wine that the doorbell rang at the Grays' house, announcing the arrival of Mark Pierce from the debate club. Evelyn answered the door in a pair of jeans and a Hard Rock Cafe, V-neck tee shirt; under which she wore her get-out-the vote bra. Though the T-shirt wasn't as revealing as her rayon blouse, the bra's structure still lifted her spirit, among other things, to enhance what nature provided.

"Hi Mark," Evelyn greeted the young man as if she had talked with him dozens of times. "I appreciate you coming over to help me with my geometry homework," she added for her brother's benefit. "Let's go into my father's study. He, uh, won't be using it tonight."

"Okay." The two teenagers entered the comfortable room where Evelyn's father sometimes worked after hours on projects for the paper supply company. The bookshelves were filled with an array of Reader's Digest condensed books, paperback romance novels that belonged to Evelyn and her mom, and sports books to represent her brother's interests.

"This is really a nice place to study," Mark said, pulling a geometry book from his backpack and noticing the convertible sofa with its plaid print.

"Oh, you didn't need to bring your book, I have one."

"Well, this is the one I use for tutoring. It's got a lot of my notes in it. What chapter are you having trouble with?"

"Eight."

"Okay," he said, coming over to the business side of the desk where she had spread out her papers and her book. He opened his book to the same chapter and set it down on top of hers. Leaning over so he could point out the lesson, and get a better look down Evelyn's T-shirt, he said, "A lot of kids get caught up right here. Is that where you're having trouble?"

"Why yes," she answered, surprised that he could go right to the problem.

"Don't feel bad, this part slowed me down too. I'll take you through it slowly," and while she concentrated on his explanation of how to divide up parallelograms into rectangles and triangles, he concentrated on the expansion and contraction of her breasts.

"Wow. You were right, I really do understand this better now, and it took less than half the time it would have if you hadn't come over," Evelyn said. "How can I thank you?"

"Well, I was wondering if you would like to go out with me. Maybe to a movie or something?"

"Oh, gee, Mark. I'm, uh, I'm seeing someone, kinda a steady guy," she lied, but conjured an image of someone that caught her attention at her brother's school. "He's a freshman at the high school. His name's Dan, Dan Miller," she stood up and faced him, but didn't look directly into his eyes.

"Oh sure, I understand. But don't you want to do stuff with other guys too? I mean you're pretty young to be tied down to just one guy. Wouldn't you like to experience different guys?" he said softly.

Looking up Evelyn noticed Mark for the first time. Behind the glasses was an attractive young man. His brown eyes had a puppy-dog look. Maybe if he did something different with his hair, got some cool frames, and got rid of the nerdy white shirt, he would look pretty good. "What kind of experience do you mean?"

"Allow me," he said like the leading man in a '40s musical. He bent toward her and kissed her lightly on the lips. Evelyn wasn't sure if she was more surprised by his bold move or the provocative feeling it gave her. Before she had time to consider the source of her surprise Mark had put his arms around her and was probing her mouth with his tongue. She had been kissed before, but never like this. She wondered if all the nerdy guys knew about this, maybe they got it out of books or something. She didn't know how he perfected his technique, but she knew she liked it.

Evelyn let her body relax against Mark's as he kneaded her back like he was preparing dough for a very delicate pastry. She let him lead her to the convertible sofa where they lighted side by side. She took his lead and began to explore his mouth with her tongue like a spelunker in a new, exotic cave. Mark moved his right hand up under her T-shirt, paid passing homage to her back and then moved it around to pay tribute to her campaign manager. A front clasp made it easy for him to release her bra, and her hard little nipples rose up to greet his nimble fingers. Between the two of them, they managed to free her from the T-shirt and bra.

Unbeknownst to the couple on the sofa, Zane was playing voyeur with the aid of the mirror in the entry hall. He had turned up the volume on the television and positioned himself in a reclining chair so he would see only faceless bodies groping and writhing, making it easier for him to ignore the fact that he was watching his sister.

Mark was keenly aware of the light perspiration that formed in the valley of Evelyn's breasts, and he wondered that if his probing fingers were a dowsing tool, where else he might find wetness. Evelyn already knew, and she both craved and feared relief. This guy knew too much, she thought. He's smart. He says all the right things. And, he knows how to turn a girl on. What should she do? On the one hand, so to speak, she wanted him to touch her. She knew he would be gentle and light. Then again, she was afraid it might go too far. She knew about AIDS and other STDs, and she knew about unwanted pregnancies. If only she could stop him after letting him please her with his hands, with his fingers—that would be okay. But what if she couldn't stop him, or herself, at that crucial junction?

In the other room, Zane had mentally pasted the face of a girl in his civics class on the half naked body being caressed. He had also removed his tumescent penis from his jeans and was working it with a practiced hand.

The better thing to do, Evelyn thought, was to stop Mark now. Now while she could still think. She could always finish the job herself, substituting her hand for his, her caressing fingers for his tongue. Oh yes, a shiver already passing through her, because he had just touched her on top of her jeans, I better stop this now, now, now…

"Mark," Evelyn whispered desperately as she pulled away from his face. "I think we better cool it."

"Oh Evelyn, you're even more beautiful and sensual than I could have imagined," his voice had found the huskiness of his leading man gestures.

Sensual, she thought. Who would have thought that a girl in junior high was sensual. But he had said it. He recognized the woman in her she always knew was there. "Mark, that's really a wonderful thing for you to feel, but everything is happening so fast. Please let me slow down a little. Maybe we can pick this up again another time?" she pulled a little farther away and noticed with pride that there was a manly lump in Mark's lap.

He followed her eyes to where his erection was straining against the twill fabric of his trousers. "See what you do for me?" he said. "It's hard for guys at this stage, we can't just turn it off."

"I'm sorry Mark. But we hardly know each other," she said, forgetting her bra and pulling her tee-shirt on in one swift motion. "You're a really nice guy, and maybe you're right about me seeing other people besides my boyfriend. Maybe we can get together again, I think I would like that," she was talking a little faster now. "Don't you think that would be a good idea? I mean, just let it be for tonight, and we can get together again. Maybe in a few days? What do you think?"

In the other room Zane had closed his eyes before his sister had covered herself. The image of her breasts and another woman's face still projected against the inside of his eyelids, he continued to stroke himself as he neared orgasm.

The softness in Mark's eyes had changed, but the hardness in his lap hadn't. "You don't understand how it is with guys when we get turned on like this," he reached out and grabbed her by her upper arm. Pulling her close so their faces were inches apart he continued, "It was probably the same thing with your dad and that girl. It just got out of hand and something had to be done to finish the job."

"Wh, uh, wh, what are you saying?" Evelyn screamed into his face, her mind reeled like the spinning up-ending ride at an amusement park. "You knew about that when you came over? You thought you could fool around with me because of what they say my father did?" She was wriggling and trying to stand, but somehow Mark kept his grip on her arm, keeping her off balance and down on the couch.

"Get out, get out," she yelled. "Zane, help. Zane, help." But in his fantasy ecstasy Zane couldn't respond immediately. He tried to shove his engorged cock back into his pants, but it hurt. He knew he couldn't go on masturbating, so he pushed hard on his dick, finally getting it back into his boxers just as nature took its course and a stream of white semen shot down his leg. Still, he got up, zipped his trousers and headed for the study.

"Hey, shithead, what are you trying to do to my sister?" Zane bellowed from the doorway, unaware that a wet streak was already changing the color of his jeans from pale blue to a dark indigo along his left thigh.

Mark looked up to see Evelyn's older brother in the doorway. He jumped to his feet and ran past Zane without even noticing the vertical wet spot that would soon dry and glue Zane's pants to his leg. Out the front door Mark ran and kept running for two blocks, his mind gingerly creating a scenario that would account for his presence at the Grays' house, in case Evelyn Gray came to school the next day accusing him of any wrong-doing.

Chapter 18

Lights out doesn't really exist in a jail. It only refers to the lights inside the cells having to be turned off. Not those in the halls that allow shadows to dance on cell walls all night as guards make their rounds and moths commit hara-kiri against hot, naked bulbs. However, the mandate for lights out came at 10:00 in the part of the jail where Earl Levy had managed to get Chuck Gray a semi-private cell.

As the over-bright surreal ambiance of jail life was dimmed to the semi-darkness of night in Gray's cell, a teenager could be seen running from the Gray's suburban home, and a late model BMW might be sighted approaching a luxurious and exclusive condominium building in the high-rent part of town.

Only moments had passed in the jail when Gray's cellmate, ensconced on the much coveted lower bunk, began breathing irregularly. It came as no surprise to Gray, the man below had just sat in the cell's only chair chain smoking for the last two hours.

The man probably had emphysema, at the very least, Gray thought. God, he might even have tuberculosis. What a thought, since TB is contagious. Gray hoped he wouldn't have to put up with the noise all night. Maybe when the man rolled over his breathing would become less labored. But, much to Gray's disappointment, it was getting even louder, and to top it off, the springs on the lower bunk were beginning to squeak.

Oh my God, Gray realized. It wasn't emphysema or TB. The man below was masturbating. Then, as if Gray's discovery had triggered the desired response, there was a final grunt and then absolute quiet below. Gray was thankful. Thankful for the quiet. Thankful that the man chose to relieve himself instead of resorting to rape.

How could anyone get turned on in this environment, Gray wondered. But the answer wasn't far away. It wasn't passion that drove his cellmate to an erotic fantasy, it was boredom and anxiety, it was an analgesic and a soporific. Guys do it all the time. As kids they do it the night before the big game or a final in a difficult class. It relieves stress and helps them sleep. Even as a married adult, there was satisfaction in mutual masturbation with his prim-appearing wife. And, there were times when only soloing would do.

He tried to think of the first time. It was a pleasant memory, though a confusing time for him. He didn't even ejaculate, at least nothing came out. He must have been about 9 or 10. He had no idea how he got the erection. He didn't know about the correlation between his admiration of a classmate's nipples—protruding from her flat chest and outlined by a red sweater—and the boner that pressed against the firm mattress of his bed. His pumping action was almost a reflex. It felt good. Then, suddenly, his pelvis jerked spasmodically, his hard little penis twitched, its pink, circumcised head seemed to inflate and deflate with the beat of his heart, and then it went limp, and he went to sleep.

It wasn't until a year or two later that this same sensation led to the sticky stream of semen shooting out between him and the sheets. He felt it with his hand. It was warm and gooey. Then it began to get cold. He was scared. He didn't know exactly what it was. Guys at school had talked about cum and jizzem, spunk and cream, shooting a wad and jacking off. This is what it must be, he thought. He hoped. And he fell asleep.

He thought about sex, with himself and with others. It was always better with others. It was at least six years before that first, dry jerking sensation until he experienced sex with another. The school slut, God bless her, he thought. While the other girls, and some of the boys, chastised Jeanne, it was she that gave of herself to bring so many boys to manhood. Of course, Gray thought/knew/wished and hoped his little Evelyn wasn't *that* kind of girl. But oh how glad he was for Jeanne. Gray's best friend Stephen, a boy with experience, had Jeanne first. It was Steve who suggested that

Jeanne initiate Gray. Oh God, he couldn't believe it, he was going to get laid at the age of sixteen, and by an expert.

Gray had screwed up his courage and bought a three pack of rubbers at the local drug store. It was a cliché. Scared shitless, he wandered the isles, picked up something banal and unnecessary, like rubbing alcohol or hydrogen peroxide, and approached the counter. Of course, it had to be the woman on duty who asked, "Will there be anything else?"

"Yes," he replied, trying to make his voice sound deeper. "A pack of Trojans." Whew, shit, he had gotten the words out. He knew it was legal to buy condoms at any age, but he just knew he would blow it. Thank God, it was over. The questions were done, the deed out there in the universe where it couldn't hurt him anymore. She would simply turn around, get the brand he asked for, ring up the sale, put his items in a sack, make change and he was out of there.

Oops, road block, crisis ahead: "Reservoir tip or plain? Lubricated or regular?"

Aaaaaah. Suddenly he could feel the lights from above pounding on his head. What was the right thing to do? Oh shit, grab the first choice and hope to hell you're right: "Reservoir. Lubricated." Did his voice really go up to a crystal-shattering pitch? Oh please God, let it just be in my ears, he thought. Meanwhile, his imaginary antagonist merely turned, retrieved his selection and concluded the transaction.

Lying on a soft, smelly mattress suspended by tired springs, Gray smiled despite himself. Kids today don't know how lucky they have it. They can go into a market, grab a package of condoms off the shelf and make it through the fast lane in a quick, uninhibited five minutes. Hell, they can even go through the self-check-out lines. Of all the things kids can have today: computers, smart phones, 1,000 channels of mediocre television, DVRs, CDs, iPods; the one thing he wished he could have had was the privilege of the uninhibited, anonymous purchase of condoms.

A bright child, Gray decided to sacrifice one of the three brave Trojans to a test run. His head swimming with pictures of Jeanne's young, firm breasts and round little bottom, he brought himself easily to an erection. Like a bag of potato chips, he ripped through the foil with his teeth, extracted the slippery piece of latex and examined it. Noting which way it was rolled up, he placed it over the head of his erect pecker and rolled it easily down the shaft. Well, as long as it was already there, he thought, and a few strokes later his semen shot into the reservoir tip. Satisfied that he had bought the right gear, he slid the used rubber off his rapidly softening penis, trashed it, pulled up his trousers and reached for the phone.

Jeanne had been primed by Stephen. She invited the young Chuck Gray to her place after school, her parents both being at work. They kissed awkwardly and dispassionately on a sofa. Chuck was all hands, trying to remove all her clothes at once. "Here, let me help," Jeanne offered. She pulled her sweater up over her head and quickly unhooked her bra. Little titties stood at attention, too small for gravity to notice, but a feast for a starving young stud.

As Chuck fondled her breasts, Jeanne shimmied out of her skirt and panties, and then started to undress him. His erection was so intense it sprang from his shorts the moment she undid his jeans. Chuck groped at Jeanne's crotch, trying to stick a finger in her dry vagina. "Slow down, Chuck, we've got plenty of time."

He tried to slow down, but hormones flowed through his body like the Indy 500. His body out of control, his erection a heavy weight on the accelerator of his desires. "I need to get wet there," she told him, and moved her hand on top of his to slow his pace and soften his touch. "This is how you should do it. You have protection, don't you?"

"Yes," he reached his other hand into the pocket of his pants on the floor. Pulling out the remaining two prophylactics, and thinking that she was ready for him, he ripped the edge off one envelope with his teeth. Then he rolled the condom on as he had done before; and then he came.

"Oh shit," he said. "I'm sorry Jeanne. I, uh, I..."

"That's okay, Chuck. Just wait a few minutes. Take that off and I'll help you get hard again."

Oh thank God for Jeanne, Gray thought in his smelly little cell, a smile on his face and the beginning of an erection growing in his pants as he relived how she sucked him to another erection, one that lasted long enough for him to truly get laid for the first time.

But his hard-on never came to fruition. Unlike his cellmate, Gray was snatched back to his present time and place like a jumper on a bungee cord. Shit, passion, he thought. Young, firm breasts and tight small asses. It started with Jeanne, those many years ago, and now it may all have ended with Felicia Tafoya.

Chapter 19

Sharleen Sicarian understood the deep restful sleep of post-orgasmic slumber. She felt good all afternoon and into the evening. It was a delight when she told her husband the news; she had helped the police apprehend a criminal. On top of her heroism, she had cornered and hobbled the comptroller, Chuck Gray. The only employee at the paper goods warehouse that still answered directly to company president Bob Benton instead of to her.

Her husband Jody was thrilled to hear the story of how she put the pieces of the puzzle together to help the police. It wasn't that he shared her enthusiasm for having Gray hauled off to the poky in front of the other employees, or her apparent feeling of importance in bringing a criminal to justice. Jody's delight came from his wife's obvious mood. He learned over the eight years of their marriage that when she felt this good about herself, he was going to reap the benefits.

Indeed, their love making had been intense and prolonged. Her outburst of, "Yes, yes, yes" might have been interpreted by another as an affirmation of herself. But Jody was a simple man, he worked hard as a telephone company employee. He did not aspire to a management position, and he did not question matters. So he accepted Sharleen's jubilation for what it appeared to be, a great orgasm in which he shared.

* * *

Bob Benton's night was one of fits and starts. No sooner would he begin to doze than some image of the last 20 years or so invaded his slumber. Chuck Gray was always there. It might have been the day Benton himself hired Chuck. A young man out of college, his first position was Accounts Payable and Payroll. A hard worker and loyal employee, it was Benton's pleasure to bestow a handsome, though useless, set of cuff links on Gray's son Zane on the occasion of the young man's bar mitzvah. Of course, he had to pony up a similarly valued gift for Gray's daughter, Evelyn, when she had her bat mitzvah, though he couldn't remember what it was.

Gray and Benton even shared an occasional luncheon where, up until the last few years, they might exchange lascivious glances and salacious comments about a waitress or a woman at another table. But Benton never thought of Gray as someone who would stray from his wife, much less attack a woman. Despite the circumstantial evidence, Benton found it hard to accept Sicarian's suspicions. Perhaps it was because Gray was the only one Benton knew who had definite knowledge of Benton's own marital infidelities. Among men, that is a bond of sacred trust.

* * *

And, on the 14th floor of an expensive condominium building in the historically significant, overpriced and recently rejuvenated part of town, Earl Levy poured two fingers of 100-year-old Grand Marnier into oversized, Waterford snifters. To June Gray, the lights seemed a little too dim for propriety, but she passed that off as the effects of the dinner wine on her senses; Earl knew better.

The aroma of the brandy was as delicate as a dream, its presence in their mouths was as quiet as a thought, and its warmth as it slithered down was like a hot python enveloping their bodies from their lips to their stomachs.

"Um, really smooth," June Gray said, missing her own double entendre.

"Glad you like it," the lawyer replied as he guided her toward the floor-to-ceiling windows that provided a to-die-for view of the city. The choreography was so perfect, the scene so well rehearsed that June Gray could only follow his lead. Their kiss ignited the brandy creating a fusion of heat in their mouths. It followed the course of the liquor, and then went beyond, exploding in her breasts, and throbbing in their loins.

"Oh my God," she exhaled.

"Oh June," he breathed.

"Earl. Earl, this isn't right."

"Yes it is. You know it is. You've known it since this morning."

"But it feels so strange. You know, with Chuck in jail. Oh God, I can't believe it. Why does he have to be in jail. It seems so, uh, surrealistic. Twenty-four hours ago we were making love passionately, and now I'm in someone else's arms, and I want to… Oh…"

Levy had just the right answer for every situation, in or out of the courtroom. His mind worked like a pinball machine with a computer inside. The question or statement would spring out of a witness's mouth like a shiny ball. It would bounce off bumpers and rails until it found its way to just the right pocket, and then he would trap it with a quick rebuttal, a scathing question, or a quiet innuendo with the edge of a stiletto.

But this time the ball just kept bouncing from rail to rail. It defied his quick wit and his encyclopedic mind. He could not reconcile what she just said with the scenario he planned. "You made love with your husband last night?"

The chill caused her to step back. "Yes. Why should that matter to you?"

Only the truth now. "The woman that was raped and murdered…"

"Yes?"

"Some of the blood they found tested positive for HIV."

The chill turned into a glacier. "Oh my God. You believe Chuck did it. You're afraid that if you fuck me tonight you'll get it. You think Chuck did it and gave me AIDS. Goddamn you. Goddamn you." She ran for the door, grabbing her purse but leaving her coat in the rush. He started for the door, paused and then pursued her. To his chagrin, the elevator was waiting patiently for her like the yawning jaws of a dark cave from which there would be no return.

Pounding the first floor button all the way down to the lobby, she quick-stepped to the entry where a very perceptive doorman hailed her a cab. And, had she known that the cab ride would be the last opportunity for peace and quiet, she would have made better use of the time. Instead she replayed her fly-like visit into the web of intrigue Earl Levy had woven.

She wished that she weren't going to be all alone when she got to her house. She wanted Chuck to be there, that is Chuck before this whole thing happened. Chuck in a comfortable pair of slacks, slippers and a favorite old shirt he wouldn't let her donate to Goodwill. Even if the kids would still be up, that would be a comfort. But they had school tomorrow and should be in bed by now.

* * *

"Oh Zane," even Evelyn was surprised at how tenderly she said his name as she hugged her brother. "Thank you. I never thought I would be so glad that you were here for me."

"It's okay, Ev. He's just a little jerk," Zane replied, trying to gently push her away.

"Yeah, but who knows what might have happened if you hadn't been here," she let him put some distance between them now that the crisis was past. "Oh, what happened to your jeans?"

"Oh. I spilled some Coke on it when you screamed. It's okay, it'll dry."

Instinctively she looked over his shoulder. She was trying to see the reflection of the spilled soda in the other room by looking at the reflection in the hall mirror. When she didn't see any glass, can or bottle, she suddenly realized that her brother had been in the other room so he could watch her. In her agitation about their father, about running for president of the debate club, about having this strange, nerdy boy in the house, she had forgotten all about the spy mirror in the entry hall. "Oh God Zane, you're sick. That's not Coke on your pants, you were watching us, weren't you? You sick sonofabitch, you were jacking off while you watched your little sister about to get raped." She turned and stomped her feet. Then turned back, hit him in the stomach and ran past him, out into the night.

"Evelyn. That's not it at all. I didn't see your face. I mean my eyes were..." But she had already disappeared into the darkness between the street lights. And, a moment later headlights turned the corner from the opposite direction, then pulled into their driveway.

June Gray lighted from the car, fumbled for some bills and pushed them through the cab's window. Without waiting for change, she took two steps toward the front door, hesitated when she saw her son, and then continued.

"Zane. How come you're still up? You should be in bed like your sister. It's a school night."

"Hi Mom. Are you okay?" he noticed her tousled hair and spotty lipstick. "How did your meeting with Dad's lawyer go?"

His question brought color to her cheeks, more anger than blush, though one would be hard pressed to tell the difference.

"Nothing was really decided," she said walking past him. "We're hoping to get your father out of there tomorrow, otherwise he might have to spend the entire weekend there.

"What's been going on here?" June demanded. A look around told her something was amiss. School books were open on her husband's desk. Cushions were akimbo on the sofa, with one completely on the floor, and the television in the other room was up way too loud.

"Uh, Ev had a friend over. They were doing homework together. And, well, he got a little fresh and she told him to leave."

"What about the TV? Why's it so loud?"

"I was watching. They were talking a lot so I turned it up."

"Uh huh," she replied with little credulity. "When did Evelyn go to bed?"

"Well, she got pissed and ran out of the house just before you drove up."

"Young man."

"Sorry, Mom. I mean she got upset and left. It was just a minute ago."

"Well, we better go find her. There's no telling what might happen to her in the middle of the night all by herself. I'm going to change into some jeans, you straighten up in here." Zane bent down without a thought and picked up the math book from the floor. As soon as he heard the door close to his mother's room, he ran up the stairs and quickly changed his pants.

A few minutes later, when June Gray descended the stairs, Zane was already back in the study putting the last of the couch cushions back into its place. "C'mon," June said as she passed the study door on her way to the car parked on the drive. "Which way did she go?"

Zane pointed up the block as he opened the passenger door of his mother's car.

"I'll drive slow, watch for your sister. She may try to duck into a bush or something if she's still upset."

"Okay, Mom."

For the next 30 minutes mother and son drove the neighborhood, methodically criss crossing streets and cruising boulevards. Finally, on the edge of a greenbelt Zane spotted his sister. She sat on the grass with her knees pressed up against chin, her arms around her calves and her blonde hair tumbling down over her face like a sheep dog. "She's over there Mom. On the grass."

June eased the car slowly over toward her daughter and parked about 50 feet from where the adolescent sat. She cut the engine, got out and let the door fall shut before walking quietly over. "Hi honey," June greeted her daughter, "heard you had a close encounter of the nerd kind?"

Evelyn didn't know what to say. Should she rat-out her brother, the teenage pervert? Should she admit to her mother that her lingerie was inappropriate, that she was having a good time until the dork mentioned her father? That she was really pissed at her father for letting his prick think for him, and getting caught and bringing shame to her? She didn't know where to begin, so when June sat on the grass next to her and put an arm around the young woman's shoulder, Evelyn just leaned into her and cried.

Chapter 20

By the time June and her kids got back to the house it really was the middle of the night. Not midnight, as most people think of it, but 2 a.m., about halfway between a 10:30 p.m. bedtime and a 6 a.m. waking. "Would you like some milk or tea?" June asked them.

"Nothing for me," Zane said, anxious to get away from his sister and the possibility of pissing her off so much she would tell their mother about his behavior.

"Can I have some milk, Mommy?" Evelyn replied, speaking for the first time since she ran from the house, and throwing out the childlike diminutive like a life saver for her mother to reel her in.

"I'll just put it in the microwave for half a minute to take the chill off. Do you want to talk about what happened this evening Evelyn?" June opened the psychological door wide for her daughter at the same time as she opened the microwave.

"Not really. It was just a bad trip. The guy's a complete jerk."

"Why do you say think so?"

"He said he would help me with geometry, but he really wanted to fool around."

"Did he think that you were the type of girl to fool around?"

"I don't know."

"Did it have anything to do with the way your dressed for school today?" June asked as she set Evelyn's milk in front of her.

"I don't know."

"What did he say to you?"

"He didn't say anything."

"He just leaned over and pulled your bra off from underneath your T-shirt?"

"No."

"Then what happened to it? You're not wearing one now."

98

"I just didn't put one on tonight. I didn't think it was necessary," Evelyn said raising the glass to her lips.

"I don't think so Evelyn. Anyone can see your nipples. Besides, your bra is still on the floor in the study. Tell me what really happened."

"It's all Dad's fault," she answered, putting the glass down hard enough on the table for milk to jump out. "Mark came over here tonight because he heard about Dad getting arrested for raping that girl."

"What could that possibly have to do with you?"

"Maybe he thinks it runs in the family. That every fucking one of us is a pervert."

"Evelyn, watch your language."

"Why should I watch my fucking language? My brother was watching me when Mark tried to rape me. Did he do anything? No fucking way. He was too busy pulling on his prick to care."

"Evelyn."

"Don't believe me? Check the hamper where his cum-stained pants are. Jesus, Mother, are you so naive? What about you, slithering out in the night with Dad's lawyer? Did you get any tonight? I almost did, and Zane certainly did." She jerked up from her seat, tipped the table, knocked over the milk glass and ran for her room as the white liquid cascaded over the edge of the table onto the vinyl-tile floor.

June felt like she had been shot with a dart. As she watched the glass fall in micro-inches and the milk run off the table like thick white molasses on a cold day, she heard her son yelling in the hall upstairs. "You little slut, why did you have to go and tell Mom? You were the one leading that little shit on, letting him feel you up and rub your crotch. I hope you get grounded for a year, you little bitch."

Two doors slammed hard upstairs while June watched the last of the milk drop to the floor like spent semen. What had she done? What did Chuck really do? Would their home ever be the same? The way it was this morning—a mere 20 hours earlier? She held her head in her hands and just cried and cried. Through her own tears she missed the sobs coming from her children upstairs. Then, when her tears were all gone, well after her children had dozed off on damp pillows, she moved zombie-like up to her room, splashed water on her face, curled up in the fetal position on her bed and fell asleep in her clothes.

* * *

Two a.m. also found officers Rossi and Taylor arriving on the scene of a reported domestic dispute. Night sticks drawn they approached a home near the airport. As they got closer they heard muffled screams coming from the backyard. Both officers exchanged night sticks for guns. Bright beams led them around the side of the house and into the yard where a man was about to mount a woman. He pushed against her shoulders forcing her face into the ground. His pulsing erection was inches away from her quivering buttocks when it was caught in the beam of a five-battery flashlight like a serpent in a side show search light.

Officer Taylor flipped her long-handled flashlight around in an instant and whacked the man's rock-hard penis with the ribbed, metal handle. He yelped like a spanked puppy, releasing his grip on the woman's head. Officer Rossi winced at the blow, but still managed to bring out handcuffs in a blink of an eye and catch one of the assailant's hands as it waved wildly in the air. In another swift motion, he brought the hand down behind the miscreant's back and matched it to the other hand.

Click-ratchet. Click-ratchet. The perp's hands fastened securely behind him, and his flailing dick waving defiantly in front of him, Rossi tipped him on his side so the two police officers could tend to the victim. The woman was young and Hispanic, and Rossi noticed, firm of breast and buttock.

"Are you all right, honey?" Taylor asked, though regardless of the woman's answer, Taylor knew in her heart the answer was a No that would resound through all the years of her life.

"I'm as well as can be expected," came the surprisingly coherent reply. "Would you mind…" she began, looking up from all fours like a wounded, female centaur.

"Rossi please," Taylor said to her partner.

"Sorry," the other officer said, turning away, grabbing the perp's collar and yanking him to his feet. His penis dangled limply in the cool night air as he shuffled away from the scene of his crime with pants and underwear hobbling his ankles.

Taylor took off her jacket and put it over the shoulders of the nearly-raped woman. Helping her to her feet, Taylor asked how she was doing.

"I'm going to be okay. Another minute and he would have penetrated me. Thank God you showed up when you did."

"What's your name? Do you live here?" Taylor asked, instinctively leading the woman to the back door of the house.

"Dolores Umberto. No, no, this is not my house. Please, let me get my clothes and things," she turned and went back to where her torn blouse and ripped jeans lay. Ignoring her bra, but pulling on panties, she did her best to cover up. "I live over on 38th. I was walking from the bus stop when this guy came at me from behind a bush. I ran down this drive hoping there was a way out."

"Why were you out so late?"

"I had been studying with a friend, we're having finals, I'm a student at State. He offered to let me stay overnight, but I didn't want him getting ideas. So I took the bus. Next time I'll let him get all the ideas he wants, but that's all he'll get is ideas."

Taylor smiled despite herself. It turned out to be the best thing she could do, there was instant rapport, and Dolores Umberto began to relax. "Hey, this is going to hit you very soon," Taylor told her. "My partner should have called for backup by now, I'll ride with you to the station where we can get your statement. When you're feeling better we'll take you right to your front door, okay?"

"Yeah. I want to see that asshole locked up so he can find out how he likes getting butt-fucked," Umberto said, and Taylor began to see the first signs of her breakdown coming.

Taylor was right. By the time she and Umberto reached the street, another squad car had pulled up. Taylor slipped into the backseat with Umberto, while the officer riding shotgun in the second car slid into the backseat of Rossi's unit with the still half-naked perp. "Jesus," the officer said to Rossi, "give me something to cover this guy up with. I don't want to ride to the station with his cock hanging out like that." Rossi went to the trunk and got a wool blanket and threw it across the perp's lap.

Chapter 21

Once they were at the police station, Taylor turned Umberto over to a female officer specially trained to work with rape victims. Even though the woman had not yet been raped, she had been violated, and was in need of medical attention for the burns around her neck and the abrasions on her hands and knees.

Taylor joined her partner Rossi in an interrogation room where the other cops had dragged the still half-naked, handcuffed perp. The man's driver's license ID'd him as Robert Thaw. He had no criminal record.

A more thorough search of his possessions turned up a Social Security card, Visa card, MasterCard, ATM and business cards, all in his name. He also had $86 and some loose change, keys to a late model Ford, a few scraps of paper with notes on them, a receipt for gas and an doctor's appointment reminder card. Nothing that appeared to be of any value.

"You know, you're going to have a tough time in court trying to convince a judge or jury that you just tripped over that woman," Taylor said. "Why don't you make it easy on yourself, save us a lot of time and aggravation and tell us why you wanted to rape that girl?"

"You wouldn't understand," Thaw spoke for the first time.

"Try me," the young woman in blue said.

He turned to Rossi, "Hey man. Do you think I could at least pull my pants up?"

"Why should we let you do that?" Taylor snapped. "The way we found you and that girl we thought you liked it when people had their pants down."

"Come on man," he still addressed Rossi, "she really can't understand, she's just trying to fuck with me."

"I wouldn't fuck with you if you were mankind's last hope of procreation," she yelled. "You're slime. You're a coward and pervert, and you got caught by two police officers with your pants down and your pathetic little prick hanging out. You better fucking tell us what you thought you were doing to that girl, or you're going to get exactly what you were about to give her."

"Hey, godamnit, I didn't do nothing to you. Leave me alone," Thaw shouted back. "I'm not going to say anything while that bitch is in here harassing me. Especially while I'm half naked," he said to Rossi.

"Why don't you let me talk with Mr. Thaw, Bonnie?" Rossi finally spoke in a quiet tone. "I think he'll be more comfortable fully clothed. So why don't you let him loose, and take the 'cuffs with you."

Without a word, but with attitude surrounding her like vigilantes at a hanging she produced a key, unlocked the handcuffs and left the room. The slam of the door punctuated her departure as well as her true feelings.

"Go ahead and pull up your pants Mr. Thaw."

"Thank you."

"Now, will you tell me what you were doing with that woman tonight?"

"Oh shit, I guess it doesn't matter now. Maybe it'll be better if you know. Maybe then it will be over sooner."

"What are you talking about? Even if you confess to trying to rape her, there would still be a trial. If you cooperate, get a good lawyer and into a program, it might not be so bad. Come on, man. It's just us two in here, you know, man to man. What were you doing there?"

"You know, all you cops are such liars. Shit, just you and me, huh? And that bitch cop plus a DA and God knows who else behind the one-way mirror. Well fuck you," he addressed the mirror. "Fuck all of you, 'cause there isn't a Goddamn thing you can do to me. There won't be any trial because I'm a dead man. That's right, I've got full-blown AIDS. And you know how I got AIDS, because I was in a car accident and needed blood. Yeah, I got it from a transfusion. And the blood for my transfusion came from a spic whore, some wetback broad that floated into our country from Mexico. She sold her own blood for a few bucks, and she fucking gave me AIDS. Now I'm dying and I can't even get laid," he breathed hard like he had just climbed a rock wall.

"So I thought I'd kill two birds with one stone," Thaw continued, breathing a little easier. "I fuck a few spic chicks and give them back what they deserve. So up the ass it goes, just to insure they'll get it too, you know, tear a little flesh between. Plus, man, maybe they'll pass it along to their boyfriends who will pass it on to more of their women. You know how they are."

Rossi's eyes were wide. This was one sick puppy he was dealing with. "How do you know the blood came from a Hispanic woman?"

"I threw around some money at the blood bank. It didn't cost much to find out, a few hundred dollars and I had her name. But she was already dead. So I couldn't get her, but I could get her sisters and brothers."

"So, there have been others?"

"Oh yeah."

"How many?"

"Dozens."

"Really," Rossi was trying to sound impressed. "When, man? Where?"

"One just last night. Over near the airport, but I fucked up with that one."

"How? Didn't you get in?" Rossi's pretense was making him sick, but he needed to continue to sound impressed.

"Oh, I got in all right. Right up the old wazoo. But she didn't get up afterwards. I think maybe I used too much force. Hah. I guess I don't know my own strength. She probably got up later though."

"No she didn't Thaw. You killed her."

* * *

"I think I've heard enough," Taylor, looking white as salt, said to the DA on the other side of the one-way mirror. "I think maybe you got the wrong guy locked up, that Gray guy. Maybe you should let him go tonight so he can get home to his family?"

"Not just yet, Bonnie. This asshole might be talking about a whole different assault. We need more information."

"You'll get it in a few more minutes, if Rossi can keep up his little act. But you know he's our guy. It's the same M.O. Hispanic female, forced rear entry with the victim on all fours, face pressed into the ground and a cord tied around her neck. What more do you need for Christ's sake? Dick prints on her ass?"

"Calm down Bonnie. I just want to make sure, okay? What if it's a coincidence, this sick sonofabitch Thaw and Gray. What if they know each other and worked together on the victim last night? Did you think about that?"

"Come on Freddie, this guy's a loner with AIDS and a grudge. Do you really think he even knows Gray? They don't live anywhere near each other. They don't work together. Their ages are 20 years apart. What do you think their connection might be?"

"Why are you so concerned about Gray?"

"He just looks like an okay guy. Besides, he reminds me of my Dad."

"Okay Taylor, I appreciate you wanting to set an innocent man free, let's just make sure he is. Tell the sarge to start processing the paperwork, but check back with me before you cut him loose, just in case."

"Thanks Freddie."

* * *

At the beginning of the half hour it would take to process the paperwork to release Chuck Gray, the middle-aged bookkeeper was having a dream. It took him back to his childhood and the retriever he raised from a puppy to a formidable 90-pound, blonde, adoring playmate. The dog used to snuggle against the back of young Chuck's legs in the winter, sharing each other's warmth and making it impossible for the boy to roll over.

In Gray's dream he knew what would come next. The alarm would sound, waking him and the slumbering canine. Then the dog would belly crawl to the head of the bed and lick Chuck on the cheek. Only the next part of his dream was new. He woke up and felt something sweaty and warm against his body. One of its appendages pressing against his buttocks.

The realization that this wasn't part of any dream hit him at the same moment that the hand covered his mouth and yanked his head back. He had already been fucked over by his co-worker and the police, and now he was going to get fucked again. He'd had it. "No, godamnit," his silent scream mumbled against the grimy hand.

Instinctively he grabbed for the hand covering his mouth as his cellmate's penis grew fat against the cheeks of his rear. Feeling the man's hard-on, Chuck Gray forced himself to dampen his instincts and to think rationally. With a sudden motion he released his hold on the man's hand and reached around behind himself fast as a bee sting and grabbed the offending appendage. He gripped it hard at the base and pulled as though trying to yank a tooth from someone's head; with much the same result.

Gray figured to get the man to release the hold he had on his mouth, so he could scream for help. However, while the effect of Gray's tortuous grip did allow his mouth to come free, the other man did the yelling for him. Lights came on throughout the cells and uniformed guards ran toward the banshee screams that pierced through Gray's skull.

At the door to Gray's cell guards merged from different directions. Guns pulled they yelled through the bars at the nearly copulating forms. "Shut the fuck up in there," one yelled. Gray seized the moment to shout back, "Get this guy off of me, he's trying to rape me."

"Hey asshole," the guard screamed back, "I don't care if you guys kill each other, just do it quietly."

"Really," Gray managed to yell as his cellmate began to pummel him, "it's him. You gotta help me."

With Gray beginning to bleed about the ears, nose and mouth, he lost his grip, "Please," came the garbled plea, like a fish learning to speak, "Please," and then he lost consciousness.

"Okay, dickhead, you killed him," the vociferous officer said to Gray's cellmate in a quiet, almost congratulatory voice. "Now get the fuck out of the bunk and stand over in the corner so we can get the body out. Now!"

The last word penetrated the cellmate's brain like a pike. He rolled his naked form over Gray's body and fell to the floor. Like a bad boy caught with his hand in the cookie jar, he shuffled over to the corner and faced the wall. One of the guards pulled his revolver before getting a key from the retractable gizmo on his belt to unlock the door. His two fellow officers entered Gray's cell and dragged the limp body from the bunk. Each wrangled an arm over his shoulder and dragged Gray from his cell, his pants still down around his knees where his assailant had pulled them.

"Please, please," each syllable stretched out like taffy and struggled to work its way through lips caked with drying blood.

"Why, the sonofabitch is still alive," the guard on Gray's left quipped. "Should we take him back to his cell?"

"Sure," the guard on Gray's right responded, torquing his body to the right as though he were about to turn back the way they had come.

"Knock it off," the third guard said. "Let's just get him into booking. It's quiet there and we can keep an eye on him. If we take him back the pederast will kill him for sure."

Chapter 22

An hour before dawn, during the darkest, coldest part of the night, a police squad car with Charles Gray—former rape and exonerated murder suspect—in the backseat, wended its way through the sleepy, middle-class neighborhood toward his home. His freedom. His salvation. Just a half hour earlier, after the blood on his face had been washed away, after a bandage had been applied to a gash over his left eye, and after a kind-hearted Bonnie Taylor told him that someone else confessed to raping and killing Felicia Tafoya, Gray had been gently placed into the backseat of a black and white.

Taylor, driving alone while her partner completed the arrest report back at the station, was telling Gray how sorry she was for the mistake. She explained that, despite what you see on television, most arrests lead to some kind of indictment. "But once in a while, something just gets screwed up," she said.

As Taylor spoke a handsome attorney was lighting from his silver BMW parked in front of the Gray residence. Earl Levy knew his actions were irrational. He should return June's coat by messenger. But, perhaps, he thought, by personally bringing it back he might save some face, redeem the composure that had fallen into the crevice created by her seismic announcement about having sex with her potentially-AIDS-infected husband.

He knocked softly on the door, hoping the burning lights on the home's main floor indicated she was still up. Perhaps brooding about her hasty retreat; which would make his planned resurrection easier. He tapped with more force after a half minute. Still no response from the bodies that lay exhausted within. He stepped back from the porch in the stillness of the somnolent neighborhood and tried to suss out which room would be hers. On the side of the house he spotted a bay window on the upper level, an architectural detail reserved for master suite bedrooms or baths. He found some small stones and, with an underhand pitch, gently guided one up toward this window. After a moment, he lobbed another stone, this time with a little more force. The third stone was poised for its mission when a silhouette approached the pane. The window glided up easily on its sash, and June Gray's head appeared.

"What the..." June sputtered through dry lips and confusion.

"I brought your coat," the words fell limp as the garment on his arm.

"Just leave it on the porch," June surprised herself with her unequivocal answer.

"June, please. At least open the door so I can give it to you personally."

"No thanks. I've had enough of what you want to give me personally."

His retort was preempted by the sound of a car pulling up to the curb. June's gaze went to the street, as did Earl Levy's. It was a black and white squad car. Had she called the police, he wondered. What the hell did they want at this hour, she asked herself.

As the car came to a halt, the back door opened and Chuck Gray emerged. Slow, purposeful and hunchback as a giant sloth, he took two steps forward before pulling himself erect like a flower reaching for sunlight. Only instead of sunlight, he was bathed in the light coming from his home. And, instead of blossoming like the announcement of spring, he felt he had emerged among the weeds. Who was this person serenading his wife at five in the morning?

He blinked to clear his vision, but his night's ordeal refused him the luxury. "Oh my God," June Gray screamed, "Chuck." She pulled her head back inside the bedroom window, narrowly missing a minor concussion, and ran for the stairs. Her scream woke the neighbors and aroused the kids. Her footsteps brought them to full wakefulness.

Levy anticipated June's path and began to move toward the front door. Something in his movement brought a glimmer of recognition to Chuck, but still not complete clarity. The front door flew open and June rushed out toward her husband. Levy held out the coat and she brushed past it like a Pony Express rider plucking mail off a stanchion.

"Oh Chuck, Chuck, are you all right? What happened? How did you get out?" June asked in rapid sequence, her words coming in staccato bursts caused by her tears and sobs.

"They found the real murderer. He confessed."

"Oh my God," she uttered as she threw herself at him.

Weak from the whole ordeal, a lack of food and sleep, and fighting off his own potential rapist, Gray crumpled under his wife's onslaught. Levy knelt next to the prostrate pair, offering his assistance as Evelyn and Zane came running from the house, still in the clothes in which they had fallen asleep.

Officer Taylor watched the homecoming with quiet satisfaction. The entire Gray family on the front lawn of their suburban home, throwing themselves at Chuck Gray as a close family friend looked on. She smiled and returned to her squad car, her job done, in more ways than one.

* * *

"Did the police call to let you know they were letting me go?" Chuck asked Levy once they had all gone into the house.

"Uh, no. I uh... "

"He was returning my coat," June inserted. "I left it at dinner. We met to discuss your case Chuck."

The kids exchanged quick glances. "Oh," Chuck said without comprehension.

"She was upset and forgot it," Levy chimed in.

"Well thanks for returning it, Earl. If you don't mind... "

"Of course, you all want to be alone. I'll call you later."

It was only after the door closed that Chuck realized the time. "He came by at five o'clock in the morning to return your coat?"

"Chuck, it isn't what you're thinking. We had dinner. He got me to go back to his place and, well, let's just say he wasn't the gentleman we thought he was."

"You mean that while I was locked up and almost raped, you were having a fancy dinner with the shyster, and he was making a pass at you?"

"Chuck, please, you're upset. Don't talk like that. It's all over. You're back, the kids are safe, and he's out of our lives. Let's just pick up where we left off before this whole nasty mess started."

"What do you mean the kids are safe? What else happened while I was in jail?"

"It's nothing dear. Everything's going to be all right."

"You really think so?" he said.

Author's Note

I hope you have, or will, enjoy reading *Innocent Bystander*. If you belong to a book club whose members would enjoy a discussion with an author, I will gladly arrange a mutually convenient time to visit by phone, Skype, FaceTime, etc.

You may contact me through my web site at http://www.StevenRBerger.com.

For more tidbits and information on *Innocent Bystander* and projects in the works, please visit http://www.StevenRBerger.com.

Thank you.

Other books from Steven R. Berger

Ursula's Yahrtzeit Candle

One of three finalists for the Colorado Authors' League prestigious Award for Best Adult Literary Fiction

Ursula Frank, an 87-year-old woman, who fled Nazi Europe meets an Hispanic youth about to join a gang and, by telling her life story, shows him a better path.

Fat Chance

The new Sebastian Wren Mystery

Journalist Sebastian Wren and the artist Adrianne Meckler join forces to resolve two deaths. One is her father, a former judge. The other an actuary. Police think suicides. They think not. Hangings? Murder? Fat pills? Is there a connection?

The 5th Estate

Honorable mention, Southern California Book Festival

When journalist Sebastian Wren is visited by the daughter of an old flame he works to solve the dual mysteries of her paternity and her mother's kidnapping.

www.ingramcontent.com/pod-product-compliance
Lightning Source LLC
LaVergne TN
LVHW011724060526
838200LV00051B/3021